A BOOK OF BROWNIES

"We can't be very far away from Fairyland,"
shouted Hop. "We must have gone miles and
miles already. Go on, brave Dragon-bird."

On they went, and on and on. But every time
they looked behind they shivered – for the black
speck was so much larger.

At last they could see quite plainly that it was
a witch sitting on a flat magic carpet that raced
through the air in a most marvellous way.

"Oh buttons and buttercups!" groaned Hop
in despair. "Fancy, to be so near Fairyland, and
yet to be so near being captured, too! Go on,
Dragon-bird; keep it up!"

Enid Blyton's
A BOOK OF
BROWNIES

MAMMOTH

First published by Newnes 1926
This edition published 1992 by Mammoth
an imprint of Mandarin Paperbacks
Michelin House, 81 Fulham Road, London SW3 6RB

Mandarin is an imprint of the Octopus Publishing Group,
a division of Reed International Books Ltd

ISBN 0 7497 0814 X

A CIP catalogue record for this title
is available from the British Library

Printed in Great Britain
by Cox & Wyman Ltd, Reading, Berkshire

CONTENTS

POEM

Hop, Skip and Jump Play a Naughty Trick

Hop, Skip and Jump were just finishing their breakfast one morning when they heard the postman rat-tatting on all the knockers down the street.

"Dear me!" said Hop. "Everybody seems to be getting a letter this morning! Perhaps *we* shall too."

The three brownies leaned out of the window of Crab-apple Cottage and watched the postman come nearer. Next door but one, rat-tat! And a large letter fell into the letter-box. Next door,

rat-tat! Another large letter, just like the first.

"I wonder whatever the letters are!" said Skip. "They're all the same, and everyone is having one, so there'll be one for us too!"

But there wasn't. The postman walked right past Crab-apple Cottage.

"Hi!" called Jump, "you've missed us out! Come back, postman!"

The postman shook his head.

"There isn't a letter for you," he said, and rat-tatted on the knocker of the cottage next door.

Well, Hop, Skip, and Jump *were* upset. No letter for them, when everyone else had one! Whoever could be writing letters and missing them out!

"Let's go and ask Gobo next door what his letter's about," said Hop.

So the three brownies hopped into Gobo's. They found him looking very pleased and excited, reading his letter out loud to Pinkie, his wife.

"What's it all about?" asked Skip.

"Listen! Just listen!" said Gobo. "It's an invitation from the King. This is what he says: 'His Majesty, the King of Fairyland, is giving a Grand Party on Thursday. Please come.'"

"Oh!" cried the brownies. "Then why haven't *we* been asked?"

Gobo looked surprised.

"Haven't you had a letter?" he asked. "Oh well, there must be a reason for it. Have you been good lately?"

"Not *very*," said Hop.

"Not *awfully*," said Skip.

"Not at all," said Jump, who was the most truthful of the three.

"Well, there you are," said Gobo, folding up his letter. "You know the King never asks bad brownies to his parties. You can't expect to be invited if you *will* be naughty."

The brownies went out crossly. They ran back into Crab-apple Cottage and sat down round the table.

"What have we done that was naughty lately?" asked Hop.

"We painted Old Mother Wimple's pig green," said Skip.

"Yes, and we got on to Gillie Brownie's cottage roof and put fireworks down her chimney," said Jump.

"And we put a bit of prickly gorse in that horrid old Wizard's bed," said Hop. "Oh dear —perhaps we *have* been a bit naughtier than usual."

"And someone's told the King," sighed Skip.

"So we've been left out of the party," groaned Jump. "Well, it serves us right!"

Everybody except the three bad brownies had got an invitation. Brownie Town was most excited.

"It's going to be a *very* grand party!" said Gobo next door, who was busy making himself a new suit. "There's going to be dancing and conjuring, and presents for everybody!"

This made Hop, Skip, and Jump feel more disappointed than ever.

"Can't we go somehow?" wondered Hop. "Can't we dress up and pretend to be someone else, not ourselves?"

"We haven't got a card to show," said Skip mournfully.

"Look, there's Gobo's wife," said Jump, pointing through the window. "What's she looking upset about? Hi, Pinkie, what's the matter?"

"Oh, a *great* disappointment," answered Pinkie. "The conjurer that the King was going to have at the party can't come after all, and the Lord High Chamberlain can't get anyone else. *Isn't* it disappointing!"

"Not so disappointing for us as for you!" said Hop. Then a great idea came to him, and he turned to Skip and Jump.

"I say!" he said, with his naughty little eyes

twinkling. "I say, couldn't we pretend we were conjurers, and get the Lord High Chamberlain to let us in to the party?"

"What a fine idea!" cried Skip and Jump in delight. "You can be the conjurer, Hop, and we'll be your assistants!"

"But what tricks shall we do?" asked Hop. "We don't know how to do any yet!"

All that morning the brownies tried to think of conjuring tricks to do at the party, but although they tried their hardest to make rabbits come out of hats, and ribbons come out of their mouths, it wasn't a bit of good, they just couldn't do it.

They were having dinner, and feeling very unhappy about everything, when a knock came at the door.

"Come in!" cried Hop.

The door opened and an old woman with green eyes looked in.

"Good afternoon," she said, "do you want to buy any magic?"

"She's a witch!" whispered Jump. "Be careful of her."

"What sort of magic?" asked Hop.

"Oh, any sort," said the witch, coming into the room. "Look here!"

She took Hop's watch, rubbed it between her

hands, blew on it, and opened her hands again. The watch was gone!

"Buttons and buttercups!" gasped Hop in astonishment. "Where's it gone to?"

"You'll find it in the teapot," said the witch.

Skip lifted the lid of the teapot, and there, sure enough, lay the watch, half covered in tea-leaves. He fished it out with a spoon. Hop was very cross.

"I call that a *silly* trick!" he said. "Why, you might have spoilt my watch!"

"Do something else, Mistress Witch," begged Jump.

"Give me your tea-cup," said the witch.

Jump gave it to her. The witch filled it full of tea, covered it with a plate, whistled on the plate, and took it off again.

"Oh," cried Jump, hardly believing his eyes, "it's full of little goldfish!"

So it was—the tiniest, prettiest little things you ever saw! The brownies thought it was wonderful.

Then the witch emptied Jump's tea into Skip's cup. And, hey presto! all the fishes vanished.

The brownies began to feel as if they were dreaming.

"If only we could do one or two tricks like that!"

sighed Hop. "Why, we could get into the King's party as easily as anything."

"Oho, so you want to go to the party, do you?" asked the witch. "Haven't you been invited?"

"No," answered Skip, and he told the witch all about it. She listened hard.

"Dear, dear!" she said at the end. "It really is a shame not to invite nice little brownies like you! Listen—if I get you into the Palace as conjurers, will you do the trick I want you to? It's a very, very special one."

"Show us it!" said the brownies, beginning to feel most excited.

The witch went outside and came back carrying a round green basket, with a yellow lid. She put it on the floor.

"Now you," she said, pointing to Hop, "jump into this basket!"

Hop jumped inside. The witch put the lid on. Then she tapped three times on the top of it and sang:

"Rimminy, romminy ray
My magic will send you away:
Rimminy, romminy ro,
Ever so far you will go!"

Skip and Jump looked at the basket. It didn't move or creak!

"Take off the lid and look inside," said the witch. Skip took off the lid, and almost fell into the basket in surprise.

"Oh!" he shouted. "Oh! Hop's gone, and the basket's empty."

So it was. There was nothing in it at all.

"Now watch," said the witch, and putting the lid on again, she began singing:

"Rimminy, romminy ray
Hear the spell and obey;
Rimminy, romminy relf,
Jump out of the basket yourself!"

Immediately the lid flew off, and out jumped Hop, looking as pleased as could be.

"Good gracious!" gasped Jump, sitting down suddenly on a chair, "where have you been, Hop?"

"In the basket all the time," said Hop.

"But you *weren't*, we looked!" said Skip.

"You couldn't have," said Hop, "or you'd have seen me!"

"We *did* look, I tell you," said Skip crossly.

"Be quiet," said the witch. "It's the magic in the basket that does the trick. Now listen—I'll lend you that basket if you'll promise to do the trick at the party in front of the King and Queen."

"Of course we will, of course we will!" cried

the brownies. "But why do you lend it to us for nothing?"

"Oh, just because I'm kind-hearted," said the witch, grinning very wide indeed. "But mind—when you've got into the basket and have vanished, and been brought back, you've got to offer to do the same thing with anyone else. Perhaps the King will offer to get into the basket, or the Queen, or the Princess!"

"My!" said Hop, "do you think they will?"

"They're almost sure to," said the witch. "So mind you let them try. But you must remember this. If any of the Royal Family get in, tap seven times, not three times, on the lid when you sing the magic verse. Three times for ordinary folk, but seven times for royalty—see?"

"Yes, we'll remember," promised Skip, "and thank you very much for lending us such a lovely trick."

When the witch had gone, leaving behind her the green basket with its yellow lid, the three brownies were tremendously excited. They began to plan their dresses for the next day, and spent all the afternoon and evening making them.

Hop looked very grand in a black velvet suit with a long red cloak and peaked hat. Skip and

Jump were dressed like pages and were just alike in bright green suits.

When the party day came they all went out very early with the magic basket and hid in a nearby wood, for they didn't want any of the brownies to see them, and guess what they were going to do.

"I hope they have lots of lovely things for tea," said Hop. "I'm getting very hungry."

"It will soon be time to go," said Skip. "Hark! There are the drums to say that the first guests have arrived!"

"Come along then," said Jump. "We'll arrive too!"

"Now remember I'm Twirly-wirly the Great Conjurer from the Land of Tiddlywinks," said Hop, "and you are my two assistants. Don't forget you've got to be polite to me and bow each time you speak to me!"

Off they went, all feeling a little nervous. But Hop, who was bigger than the others and rather fat, looked so grand in his red cloak, that Skip and Jump soon began to feel nobody could possibly guess their secret.

At last they reached the Palace Gates.

"Your cards," said the sentry to Hop, Skip, and Jump.

"I am Twirly-wirly, the Great Conjurer from the

Land of Tiddlywinks," said Hop, in such a grand voice that Skip and Jump wanted to laugh. "I am here to take the place of the conjurer who could not come."

The sentry let them pass.

"Go straight up the drive," he said, "and at the top of the first flight of steps you will find the Lord High Chamberlain."

The three brownies went on. Hop was enjoying himself. He told the others to walk behind him, and bow to him whenever they saw him turn their way.

"You're getting a great deal too grand," grumbled Jump, who began to wish he was the conjurer instead of Hop, for he was carrying the basket and finding it rather heavy.

The Lord High Chamberlain was very surprised to see them. He was even more surprised when he heard Hop telling him who he was.

"Twirly-wirly, the Great Conjurer," he said, pretending to know all about him. "Dear me, what an honour to be sure! Very kind of you to have come, *very* kind. Pray come this way!"

He led them to a tea-table and gave Hop a chair. Skip and Jump stood behind him, and looked longingly at the cakes and jellies, tarts and custards spread out on the table in front of Hop.

Little pages ran up and offered all the nicest things to the conjurer. He took some of each, and Skip and Jump looked on enviously.

"Aren't *we* going to have any?" whispered Skip in Hop's ear. "You're not going to leave us out, are you?"

"Hush!" said Hop. "You are only my servants to-day. If you don't keep quiet I shall keep turning round to you and you'll have to bow till your backs ache!"

Hop had an enormous tea. Then he announced to the Lord High Chamberlain that he would now come and do his famous trick with his magic basket, if Their Majesties the King and Queen would like to see it.

Their Majesties at once sent a message to say they would be very pleased to see it.

"Come this way," said the Chamberlain, and led the three brownies to where the King and Queen sat on their thrones. In front of them was a square piece of grass, and round it sat scores of fairies and gnomes, brownies and elves, all waiting to see Twirly-wirly the Great Conjurer.

Hop stepped grandly up to the King and Queen, and bowed three times. So did Skip and Jump.

"I will now do my wonderful basket trick," said

18

Hop in a very loud and haughty voice. Then he turned to Skip.

"Bring me the basket," he ordered. Skip rushed forward with it in such a hurry that he tumbled over, and everyone began laughing. Jump helped him up, and together they picked up the magic basket.

"Get into it," commanded Hop, pointing at Skip. Skip jumped in.

"Put the lid on!" Hop commanded Jump. Jump did so. Then Hop tapped three times on the lid and sang:

"Rimminy, romminy ray
My magic will send you away;
Rimminy, romminy ro,
Ever so far you will go!"

Everybody listened and watched, and wondered what was going to happen. The King and Queen bent forward to get a better view, and the little Princess Peronel stood up in her excitement.

"Take the lid off!" ordered Hop.

Jump took the lid off. The basket was empty!

"Ooh!" said everyone in the greatest surprise. "Ooh! he's gone!"

"Roll the basket round for everyone to see that it's empty," commanded Hop, who was now thoroughly enjoying himself.

Jump rolled the basket round so that everyone could have a good look. Then he brought it back to Hop.

"Put the lid on!" said Hop. Jump put it on. Everybody stopped breathing, to see whatever was going to happen next.

Hop tapped three times on the lid and sang the magic song:

"Rimminy, romminy ray
Hear the spell and obey;
Rimminy, romminy relf,
Jump out of the basket yourself!"

Just as he finished the lid flew off, and out jumped Skip in his little green suit, looking as perky as anything! He capered about, and bowed to everyone.

"Oh look! Oh look! He's come back again!" shouted the fairies and brownies. "Oh, what a wonderful trick! Do it again, do it again!"

Hop bowed very low. "Would anyone care to come and get into the basket?" he asked. "I will do the trick with anyone."

"Oh let *me*, let *me!*" cried a little silvery voice, and who should come running on to the grass but the Princess Peronel!

"Come back, Peronel!" cried the King. "You're not to get into that basket!"

"Oh please, oh please," she begged. "It's my birthday and you *said* I could have anything I wanted!"

"No, no!" said the Queen, "you mustn't get into that basket! Come back!"

"I shall cry then!" said Peronel, screwing up her pretty little face.

"Oh dear, oh dear!" said the King, who couldn't bear to see Peronel cry.

"You'd better have your own way, then, but make haste about it!"

Peronel jumped into the green basket, and Skip clapped on the lid. Hop remembered what the witch had told him—he must tap the lid seven times for royalty. So, very solemnly, he did so. Then he and Skip and Jump all chanted the magic rhyme together:

"Rimminy, romminy ray,
　My magic will send you away;
　Rimminy, romminy ro,
　Ever so far you will go."

But, oh dear, oh dear, oh dear! Whatever *do* you think happened?

Why, just as the magic rhyme was finished, the basket rose into the air, and sailed right away! Higher and higher it went, over the trees and over the palace, towards the setting sun.

"Oh! oh!" cried the Queen, jumping up in terrible distress. "Where's my Peronel gone to? Bring her back, quickly!"

But Hop, Skip, and Jump were just as surprised as anyone! What an extraordinary thing for the basket to do!

"Arrest those conjurers!" suddenly said the King in an awful voice.

Six soldiers at once ran up and clapped their hands on the brownies' shoulders.

"Now unless you bring Peronel back *at once*," said the King, "you go straight to prison, and I'll have your heads cut off in the morning!"

"Oh no, no!" cried the brownies, very frightened indeed. "Please, please, we aren't conjurers! Only just brownies!"

"Nonsense!" stormed the King. "Ordinary brownies can't do tricks like that! Now then, are you going to bring Peronel back again?"

"I can't, I can't," wailed Hop, big tears beginning to pour down his cheeks. "I'm only a naughty brownie dressed up like a conjurer, because you didn't ask me to your party!"

Suddenly a watching brownie gave a shout of surprise. It was Gobo. He ran up to Hop and pulled off his peaked hat and red cloak.

"Why, it's Hop!" he cried, in astonishment.

"Your Majesty, these brownies are Hop, Skip, and Jump, the three naughty brownies of our town!"

"Good gracious!" said the King, in a terrible upset, "this is more serious than I thought. If they are really brownies, then they cannot bring back Peronel. But where did you get the basket from?" he asked Hop sternly.

Hop dried his eyes and told the King all about the witch's visit, and how she had left the basket with them.

"Oh, it's Witch Green-eyes!" groaned the King. "She's often vowed to steal Peronel away, and now she's done it through you, you naughty, stupid little brownies."

"My goodness!" said Hop, "do you think the witch has *really* stolen her for always?"

"Yes!" sobbed the Queen, who was terribly distressed. "We shall never get her back again, the darling!"

"Oh my goodness!" said Skip, in a frightened voice.

"Oh my goodness!" wailed Jump, in a miserable voice.

"Oh your goodness!" suddenly roared the King in a temper. "What do you mean, oh your *goodness!* You ought to say 'Oh your badness,' you mischievous little brownies! You haven't a bit of goodness among the three of you. And now see what you've done! I've a good mind to cut off your heads!"

"Oh my goodness!" wept Hop again. He didn't mean to say it, but he couldn't think of anything else.

The King grew angrier than ever.

"Where *is* your goodness?" he demanded.

"Yes, where *is* it?" shouted everybody.

"We d-d-don't know," stammered the brownies in dismay.

"Well, go and find it!" stormed the King. "Go along! Go right out of Fairyland, and don't come back till you've found your goodness that you keep talking about! Make haste before I cut off your heads!"

"Oh, oh, oh!" cried the three brownies in a great fright, and they all took to their heels and fled. Down the steps they went and down the drive, and out through the palace gates past the astonished sentries.

Even then they didn't stop. They rushed down the road, and into the Cuckoo Wood as if a thousand soldiers were after them!

At last, out of breath, tired and unhappy, they sat down under a big oak tree.

"Oh my goodness!" began Hop.

"Don't be silly!" said Skip. "*Don't* keep saying that. We're in a terrible, terrible fix."

"To be turned out of Fairyland!" wept Jump. "Oh what a terrible punishment! And how can we find our goodness? Of course we never shall! People don't have goodness they can find!"

"It's just the King's way of banishing us from Fairyland altogether," wept Hop. "He knows we'll never be able to go back. And, oh dear, whatever's happened to poor little Peronel?"

What indeed? None of the brownies knew, and they were very unhappy.

"The only thing to do now is to go and see if we can find Peronel and rescue her," said Jump. "We'll sleep here for the night, and start off in the morning, on our way to Witchland."

So all night long they slept beneath the big oak tree, and dreamed of horrid magic baskets, and packets of goodness that would keep running away from them.

Their Adventure in the Cottage Without a Door

Next morning the brownies set out on their journey. They soon passed the borders of Fairyland, and found themselves in the Lands Outside. For a long, long time they walked, and met nobody at all.

"I *am* getting hungry!" sighed Hop.

"So am I!" said Skip.

"Well, look! There's a cottage," said Jump. "We'll go and ask if we can have something to eat. Have you got any money, Hop?"

Hop felt in his pockets.

"Not a penny," he answered.

"Oh dear, nor have I," said Skip.

"What *are* we to do then?" asked Jump. "Perhaps there's someone kind living in the cottage, who will give us some breakfast for nothing."

The three brownies went up to the little cottage. It was surrounded by trees, and its front door was painted a very beautiful bright blue.

Hop knocked loudly.

"Who is knocking at my door?" asked a deep voice.

"Three hungry brownies," answered Hop boldly.

"Come in!" said the voice.

Hop opened the door and the brownies went in.

Clap! The door swung to behind them, and made them jump. Hop looked round to see who had shut the door.

But to his enormous surprise, he could see no door at all—and yet they had just come in by one.

"Good gracious!" he cried, "wherever has the door gone!"

"He, he!" chuckled a deep voice. "It's gone where *you* won't find it! I've got you prisoners now. Three nice little servants to work for me all day!"

Hop, Skip, and Jump looked most astonished. This was a fine sort of welcome!

Then they saw an old bent wizard, huddled up by the cottage fire, laughing at them.

"We're not your prisoners, so please let us go," said Hop.

"All right, go!" laughed the wizard.

But search as they would, the brownies couldn't find any door at all. There were blank walls all round them. Then they knew that they were prisoners indeed.

"Now, listen," said the wizard: "I will give you

your meals, and in return you must work for me. I have a great many spells I want copied out. Sit down at that table and begin work at once."

The three brownies obeyed. They knew that it was best not to anger such a powerful wizard.

He brought them each a great book of magic, and set it down beside them.

"Begin at page one," he said, "and if you make me a fair copy of all the books, without one single mistake, perhaps I will let you go."

"Oh dear!" groaned Jump, "why, the books have got about a thousand pages each."

The three brownies set to work, and very difficult it was too, for the wizard wrote so badly that they could hardly read his writing in the big magic books.

All day they wrote, and all the wizard gave them to eat was a large turnip, which tasted just like indiarubber. The brownies kept looking round to see if the door came back again; but alas it didn't.

That night, when the wizard was snoring on his bed, the three brownies began whispering together.

"We *must* escape somehow!" said Hop.

"But how?" whispered Skip and Jump.

None of them could think of a plan at all.

"It's no good thinking of escaping until we find out about that disappearing door!" groaned Hop. "The wizard's barred the window right across. We'd better go to sleep."

So off to sleep they went, and were wakened up very early the next morning by the wizard, who wanted his breakfast.

After that they had to sit down and copy out the magic books again. It was dreadfully dull work.

But suddenly Hop found he was copying out something that made his heart beat with excitement. It was about Disappearing Doors.

"A Disappearing Door will come back if a wizard's green stick is swung three times in the air and dropped," said the book. Hop's hand shook as he copied it out.

"If only the wizard's stick is green, and I could get hold of it whilst he's asleep!" he thought.

He turned round to look at the stick. Yes, it was green, sure enough—but the wizard was holding it tightly in his hand.

"But when he's asleep, he'll put it down!" thought Hop, longing to tell Skip and Jump what he had discovered.

That night he watched the wizard carefully—but oh, how disappointed he was to see that he went to bed with his stick still held in his hand.

"I'd be sure to wake him if I tried to get his stick!" thought Hop, and he whispered to Skip and Jump all that he had thought of during the day.

They were most excited. "Oh, do let's try to get his stick!" whispered Skip. "If only we could get out of this horrid cottage!"

"And if only we could go back to dear old Fairyland!" whispered Jump, with tears in his eyes.

Now Hop was the bravest of the brownies, and he couldn't bear to see Jump crying.

"I'll go and see if I can possibly get the stick!" he said. "Stay here and don't make a sound."

Then the brave little brownie crept quietly across the floor till he reached the wizard's bed.

"Snore—snore!" went the wizard. "Snore-snore!"

Carefully Hop put up his hand and felt in the bedclothes for the green stick. But oh my! No sooner did he catch hold of it, than what do you think happened?

Why, that stick jumped straight out of bed by itself, and began to chase poor Hop all round the room, rapping him on his knuckles, and hitting

him on the back till Hop began to yell in pain and fright.

That woke the wizard up. He sat up in bed and chuckled.

"He, he!" he laughed, "so you were trying to steal my stick, were you! Well, well! you won't do it again in a hurry!"

Poor Hop was running all over the place trying to get out of the way of the stick, which chased him into corners and gave him as good a whipping as he'd ever had in his life.

"Come back, stick!" at last said the wizard, and the stick jumped back into bed with him. Hop ran over to the others.

"This all comes of our last naughty trick at the

King's Palace," he sobbed. "If only we could go back to Brownie Town, I'd never be bad again!"

After that the brownies knew it was no good trying to get the stick away from the wizard. They were much too afraid of it.

"We must think of something else," sighed Skip.

Each night the brownies whispered together, but no plans could they think of at all. Then one day the wizard had a visitor.

He was a red goblin, and the ugliest little fellow you could think of. He didn't come in by the vanished door, nor by the window, so the brownies thought he must have jumped down the chimney.

"Good morning," he said to the wizard. "Have you those spells you were going to give me?"

"They are not ready yet," answered the wizard, so humbly and politely that the brownies pricked up their ears.

"Oh, ho," they thought, "this red goblin must be someone more powerful than the wizard, for the wizard seems quite frightened of him!"

"Not ready!" growled the goblin. "Well, see that they are ready by to-morrow, or I'll spirit you away to the highest mountain in the world."

The wizard shivered and shook and told the

goblin he would be sure to have the spells ready by the next day.

"Mind you do," said the goblin, and jumped straight up the chimney.

The brownies stared open-mouthed. Then Hop had a wonderful idea. He turned to the wizard.

"That goblin is much cleverer than you, isn't he?" he said.

"Pooh!" growled the wizard, angrily. "I can do things he can't do."

"Can you really?" asked Hop, opening his eyes very wide. "What can you do?"

"Well, I can make myself as big as a giant!" said the wizard.

"That's a wonderful thing," said Hop. "Let's see you do it!"

"Yes, let's," said Skip and Jump, seeing that Hop was following out an idea he had suddenly thought of.

The wizard muttered a few words, and rubbed his forehead with some ointment out of a purple box. All at once he began to grow enormously big. Bump! His head touched the ceiling, so the wizard sat down on the floor. Still he went on growing, until once again his head touched the ceiling, and he filled the cottage from wall to wall.

The three brownies had to jump on the window-sill to get out of his way.

"Wonderful! wonderful!" cried Hop, clapping his hands. "You're a giant now!"

The wizard looked pleased. He muttered something else, and quickly grew smaller till he reached his own size again.

"He, he!" he said. "That will teach you to say that the goblin is cleverer than I am!"

"Oh, but perhaps the goblin can make himself *smaller* than you can!" said Hop.

The wizard snorted crossly.

"That he can't!" he said. "Why, I can make myself small enough to sit in that pudding-basin!"

"Surely not!" said Hop, Skip, and Jump together.

"I'll just show you!" said the wizard. He rubbed some ointment on his forehead out of a yellow box. At once he began to shrink!

Smaller and smaller he grew until he was the size of a doll.

"Put me on the table!" he squeaked to the brownie. Skip put him there. He jumped into the pudding-basin and sat down.

"Wonderful, wonderful!" cried Hop. "You can't grow any smaller, of course!"

"That I can!" squeaked the wizard.

"Small enough to sit in a tea-cup?" asked Hop. The wizard rubbed some more ointment on his forehead. He grew smaller still, and jumped into a tea-cup.

"Simply marvellous!" said Hop, Skip, and Jump.

"I can grow smaller still," squeaked the wizard.

"What, small enough to creep into this wee bottle?" asked Hop, pretending to be greatly surprised, and holding out a tiny bottle.

The wizard laughed, and at once became very tiny indeed—so tiny that he was able to creep through the neck of the little bottle and sit in it easily.

Then, quick as a flash, Hop picked up the cork and corked up the bottle!

"Ha!" he cried, in the greatest excitement, "now I've got you! Now you can't get out! Now you can't get out!"

The wizard shouted and yelled in his bottle, and struggled and kicked against the cork, but it wasn't a bit of good, not a bit.

"You're a wicked wizard," said Skip, "and now you've got your punishment!"

"Where's the wizard's stick?" asked Jump, looking round. "Oh, there it is, leaning by his chair. Perhaps the wizard is powerless now and his stick will be harmless to us!"

He picked it up. It did nothing at all, but behaved just like an ordinary stick.

"Now to get out of here!" said Jump.

He swung the green stick three times into the air, and then let it fall on the ground.

At once the blue door appeared in one of the walls.

"Hurrah!" cried Skip, and flung it open. "Now we're free again!"

But, dear me! what a surprise they got when they ran out of the cottage—for, instead of being among the trees in the wood, it now stood on a sandy beach, and in front of the three brownies stretched a calm blue sea!

"Good gracious!" cried the brownies. "What an extraordinary thing! The cottage must have been travelling for days!"

They looked out over the blue sea. Not a sail was to be seen.

"Well, I don't want to go exploring along this part of the country any more," said Jump, "in case we meet any more unpleasant wizards. I wish we could sail away on the sea!"

"I know," cried Hop, "let's get the table out of the cottage, and turn it upside down!"

"And use the table-cloth for a sail!" shouted Skip, "and the magic stick for a mast!"

So into the cottage they went again, and dragged out the big table. They turned it upside down on the water, and it floated beautifully. Then they set up the mast and fastened the table-cloth for a sail.

"Bring some of that purple and yellow ointment!" called Hop to Skip. "It might come in useful!"

So the two boxes of ointment were fetched, and Hop put them into his pocket. Then, picking up the bottle with the angry little wizard inside, he pushed off their table-boat, jumped on it, and there were the brownies safe and sound on the calm, blue sea.

A tiny little breeze took them along, and they watched the wizard's cottage grow smaller and smaller in the distance.

"We'll keep the wizard with us," said Hop. "He might come in useful somehow, and so long as he's corked in the bottle, he's quite harmless."

So he slipped the little bottle into his pocket along with the boxes of ointment.

On and on they went, rocking softly over the sea, till one by one they grew drowsy, and soon in the afternoon sun they fell asleep, whilst their queer little boat went sailing dreamily on.

Their Adventure in the Castle of the Red Goblin

As THE sun was setting, the three brownies awoke and rubbed their eyes.

The sea was still very calm. Hop looked all round. Then he pointed excitedly to the left.

"Look!" he cried, "land!"

Skip and Jump looked.

"An island!" said Skip. "I wonder who lives there."

"That's a very grand castle on the top of that hill," said Jump. "Someone grand must live there, I think."

"Well, it isn't a very big island," said Hop. "What about landing, and seeing if we can find anyone and get something to eat?"

Just as he said that, the table-boat changed its course and floated with the tide towards the island.

"Good!" said Skip, "the boat thinks it would like to visit there!" and he patted the table kindly.

As they floated nearer they saw that there were trees near the edge of the sea, and directly behind them rose the steep hill on the top of which was set the castle. It was built of red stone, and gleamed oddly in the setting sun.

"I don't much like the look of it," said Hop suddenly. "Goodness knows who lives there! Don't let's go!"

But Jump was curious to see what was on the little lonely island.

"Oh, let's go!" he begged. "I tell you what we'll do—we'll just land for a few minutes, and have a look round. Then if we see anything we don't like, we'll jump on to our table-boat again, and sail off!"

"All right," said Hop, "only don't blame *me* if anything happens."

The boat reached the shingle and grated against the stones. Off jumped the three brownies, pulled their boat higher up the beach and looked round.

No one was there at all. The trees grew right down to the beach, and whispered and sighed, as if they could tell many secrets, if only they knew the brownie language.

The brownies went into the wood. It was gloomy there. No birds sang, and no little animals frisked and rustled about. Hop, Skip, and Jump thought it was a horrid place.

Then suddenly they heard the sound of crying.

"Whoever's that?" said Hop, peering between the whispering trees.

"Look! It's a little girl!" said Jump, in the

greatest astonishment. "Whatever is she doing here?"

"She's lame," said Skip. She can't walk properly."

"Let's go and comfort her," said Hop, who couldn't bear to see anyone cry.

So very quietly they walked through the trees towards the little girl. She had sea-blue eyes, golden hair that floated around her, and a dress made of tight-fitting scales, just like a fish's coat. Her feet were big and ugly.

"What's the matter, little girl?" asked Hop in his kindest voice.

The little girl jumped. She looked up at him in fright, and then stared at him and the other brownies in astonishment.

"Oh!" she said, "brownies, however did *you* come here, to this dreadful island?"

"Dreadful island!" said Skip, feeling rather uncomfortable. "Why is it dreadful?"

"Oh, don't you know who it belongs to?" asked the little girl. "It belongs to that horrid red goblin, and he's so powerful he can work nearly all the magic spells there are."

"Oh my!" said the three brownies, feeling very upset indeed. "The red goblin! Oh my!"

"It was he who came and frightened the wizard

so much!" said Hop. "Fancy having the bad luck to float to his island! We'd better sail away quickly!"

Then he turned to the little girl.

"But how is it *you're* here?" he asked, "and what were you crying for?"

"Well, I don't belong here," she said sadly. "I'm a little mermaid really, and I used to have a tail. Then one day the red goblin caught me and changed my tail into these horrid feet, because he knew I wouldn't be able to swim away then. And I've been here a whole year, keeping his red castle clean for him. Oh dear, oh dear!"

She began to cry again. Hop couldn't bear it. He put his arm round her.

"Never mind!" he said. "I'll tell you something

41

lovely. We've got a boat on the beach near here, and we'll take you away from this horrid island this very night!"

"Oh! oh! oh! how lovely!" cried the little mermaid, and clapped her hands so loudly that the brownies were afraid someone would hear.

"Come along!" said Skip, nervously. "The sun's gone down, but the moon's coming up, and there's quite enough light to set off on our voyage again. *Do* come on!"

"Yes, quick!" said Jump. And the three brownies and mermaid made their way through the trees to the shore. They looked along the beach for their boat—but, oh dear me—where *was* their boat?

It was gone. Quite gone.

"Buttons and buttercups! Where's the boat gone?" whispered Hop, feeling his heart beat very fast.

"Look!" said Skip in dismay, "the tide's taken it out to sea again! There it is, ever so far out!"

Sure enough it was. The three brownies stared at the table bobbing far away in the moonlight.

"We can swim out to it!" said Jump.

"But the mermaid can't swim now she hasn't got a tail," said Hop, "and we can't leave her alone here."

"No, we can't!" said Skip and Jump decidedly.

"But whatever *shall* we do!" wondered Hop.

"Come back to my cottage for the night," said the mermaid. "And in the morning perhaps we shall think of something."

She led them through the trees to a little tumble-down hut and gave them dry bracken to lie on for a bed. Then she made some bread-and-milk, and they all ate it and tried to think of a plan.

But soon they felt so sleepy that their eyes closed, and they slept on their bracken beds until morning.

No one had thought of a plan. Hop frowned and wondered what to do. At last he made up his mind.

"There's nothing for it but boldness," he said. "We must just march up to the castle, and demand a boat to take us away."

"That would never do," said the mermaid. "The red goblin would laugh at you and turn you into beetles or something. He's only polite to wizards, and that's because he thinks they know a magic spell that he doesn't know!"

"Very well then," said Hop, an idea coming into his head. "If he's only polite to wizards, we'll pretend to be wizards, and trust to luck to get away *somehow*. Don't talk to me for a minute, and I'll think of a plan."

Everybody was very quiet whilst Hop thought hard.

"Listen," he said. "We'll all go up to the castle with the mermaid. She must hide you two somewhere in the castle. I'll meet the red goblin alone, and if he's nasty, I'll clap my hands three times, and you must come running in. He'll think then I've called you by magic, for he won't know where you've come from—and perhaps he'll be polite then and hope to get some new spells from me!"

So it was arranged. The mermaid led them up to the back door of the castle by a secret way through the woods. Then she went to see what the red goblin was doing.

"It's all right," she whispered, when she came back. "He's having a bath. I'll take Skip and Jump into the big hall, and hide them each in a chest there. The goblin *will* be surprised when they jump out! You go round to the castle door and ring the big bell in ten minutes' time, Hop!"

Skip and Jump crept off with the mermaid, feeling very nervous indeed. She put them safely into two chests and closed the lids.

Then Hop went boldly round to the castle door. He saw a great bell-rope hanging by the side. He took hold of it and pulled it sharply three times.

Jangle-jangle-jangle, it went. Hop waited.

"Who's there?" came the angry voice of the red goblin, and the great castle door slid open, to show the goblin standing in the doorway.

"A wizard come to see you!" said Hop, bowing low.

"Come in," growled the goblin, and led the way into the great hall.

"Who are you?" he asked.

"Ah, that is a secret," answered Hop.

"Oh!" said the goblin, wondering who he could be. "How did you get here?"

"That also is a secret!" answered Hop. "I do not give my magic spells away for nothing!"

"Ho," said the goblin again, thinking this must be a very clever wizard. "Will you stay here for a day or two, and perhaps we can exchange spells?"

"Certainly!" answered Hop. "Allow me to call my servants to wait on me!"

He clapped his hands three times, and, to the goblin's tremendous astonishment, up popped the lids of two chests near by, and out jumped two brownies. They ran up to Hop and bowed.

"Master, we come from the ends of the earth to greet you," they said.

45

"How did they come into those chests then?" demanded the astonished goblin.

"That is a secret," smiled Hop.

The goblin thought there were a great deal too many secrets about this peculiar wizard. He was quite determined to find them all out.

"Come to breakfast," he said, and invited Hop to a big table on which were set all kinds of food. Hop sat down. He was very hungry, and he knew Skip and Jump were too. How could he manage to get them food?

"Servants, get under the table," he said suddenly. "Take off my shoes, and tickle my feet whilst I eat."

The goblin stared in surprise.

"I enjoy my food better when my feet are tickled," explained Hop.

The goblin said nothing, but he thought this wizard was one of the queerest he had ever met. He was astonished, too, at the way he ate. No sooner was his plate full than it was empty! He didn't know that half of it was dropped down to Skip and Jump under the table.

"Dear me!" he said at last, when Hop had taken three apples and apparently eaten them in one minute. "Tickling your feet seems to give you a great appetite, Sir Wizard."

"You should try it too," answered Hop. "Take off his boots, servants, and tickle him!"

In a second Skip and Jump slipped off the goblin's shoes and began tickling his feet. The goblin gave one yell, and fell off his chair.

"Don't, I can't bear it!" he shouted, rolling about on the floor. Skip and Jump giggled, and tickled him all the more.

Suddenly, to Hop's horror, the red goblin gave a yell of rage and shouted some magic words. Immediately Skip and Jump disappeared, and in their places were two brown mice!

"How dare you let your servants do that!" raged the goblin. "See how I have punished them!"

Hop went pale with fear. Poor Skip and Jump changed into mice! Then he faced the goblin.

"Change my servants back at once," he commanded in his biggest voice.

The goblin laughed.

"Change them back yourself, if you're such a wonderful wizard," he grinned.

Hop looked round wildly for something to help him. Then he quickly put his hand into his pocket – yes, the little bottle with the wizard in it was still there.

"Do you know what I do to people who annoy

47

me?" he asked the goblin. "I don't change them into mice—that's a *very* ordinary trick—I put them into bottles like this!"

And he drew out the bottle, and showed it to the goblin. The goblin looked at it and saw the wizard sitting inside.

"Ow!" he cried, "it's the wizard I visited yesterday! Good gracious! Look at him! As small as a beetle, sitting in one of his own bottles. Oh, what a wonderful wizard *you* must be to have done that to him!"

"Yes, I *am*!" said Hop, "and I'll put *you* into a smaller bottle if you don't do what I say! Change my servants back to their own form!"

The goblin muttered some magic words, and the two mice disappeared. In their place stood Skip and Jump again, looking as frightened as could be!

"Thank you," said Hop. "I'm glad I didn't have to bottle you up. You'd have made the fifty-fifth bottled person in my cupboard at home, if I had!"

The goblin trembled.

"Of course I don't wonder that you bottled up *that* wizard," he said. "He's a nasty little person! Not a bit truthful, and *very* stupid!"

The wizard inside the bottle heard what he said,

and was as angry as anything. He jumped about in his bottle, and kicked and struggled, and shook his tiny fist at the goblin.

"Ha, ha!" said the goblin, "you can't get at me, you tiny little thing! I always thought you were silly and stupid, but I really didn't think you were stupid enough to get put into a *bottle*!"

The tiny wizard grew so angry that Hop began to be afraid he would break the bottle, so he hastily slipped him into his pocket again.

"Now," said the goblin, "let me show you round my castle. I collect all sorts of magic things, and they may interest you."

Hop thought they certainly would, and he went with the goblin.

He was shown all kinds of things.

"This," said the goblin, "is a witch's cauldron. I can make powerful magic in it. And this is a fairy's wand. I stole it from a sleeping fairy one day."

Hop thought he was an even nastier goblin than he had thought before. But he said nothing. He just looked, and wondered if he would be shown anything that might help them to escape.

The goblin showed him his magic books, which read themselves out loud—magic seeds that grew shoots, leaves, flowers and fruit, whilst you watched—magic table-cloths that spread themselves with food. Hop began to feel quite dizzy with all the wonders shown him.

Then he saw something that made his heart beat fast.

"This," said the goblin proudly, "is a witch's broomstick!"

"Will it fly?" asked Hop.

"Oh yes," said the goblin. "But it only flies when you say the magic words—and that's a secret —ho, ho!"

"Pooh!" said Hop, "you only say it's a secret, because you can't make it fly, or you don't want me to know you can't! *You* don't know the magic rhyme!"

"I do, then!" cried the goblin, in a temper. "Listen:

> Onaby O
> Away we go,
> Onaby Eye
> Up in the sky!"

Immediately the broom rose in the air, and flew towards the window. The goblin clapped his hands. It flew back again, and stood still in its place.

"There you are," said the goblin. "Did I know the magic rhyme or didn't I?"

"You did!" said Hop, grinning to himself to think that he and Skip and Jump now knew it too. "I beg your pardon. You are cleverer than I thought."

That pleased the goblin, and he became quite friendly. After dinner he went away by himself to practise magic, and Hop, Skip, Jump, and the mermaid went to the kitchen to make their plans.

"We'll creep to-night into the room where the broomstick is," planned Hop, "and jump on it. We'll say the magic rhyme, and off we'll go."

They wandered about the castle till night fell. Then, when the goblin had shown them their room, and bade them good night, they crept to the kitchen again to fetch the mermaid. Then Hop went to see if the way was clear.

He tiptoed into the room where the broom was kept—but, oh my! There was a light there, and the red goblin was sitting at the table, reading a magic book.

"He may be there all night," sighed the mermaid.

"Well, we *must* go to-night," decided Hop, "because any minute tomorrow I might give myself away; I nearly did lots of times to-day."

Just at that moment he felt the little bottle in

his pocket jerking about. He took it out, and saw the tiny wizard knocking on the glass.

"Let me out!" he squeaked in a voice like a mouse, "let me out! Let me get at that red goblin."

"Well now, that's an idea!" said Hop, staring at him.

He ran up into the room above the one in which the red goblin sat, and kicked and thumped on the floor, and made a terrible noise. Then he loosened the cork in the wizard's bottle, and set the bottle down in the middle of the floor. Then he ran and hid behind a curtain.

After a bit up came the red goblin, wondering whatever in the world all the bumping and thumping was. He was very much surprised to see the bottle on the floor. He went up and looked at it.

Directly the wizard saw him, he began kicking and banging at the loosened cork. Then Pop! out it flew, and out came the wizard like a beetle on the floor. In a trice he grew bigger and bigger, until he reached his usual size.

And then, oh my! He went for the red goblin and gave him a terrible punch in the chest. The goblin went over like a skittle.

Hop didn't wait to see any more. He ran downstairs and called the others. Together they went into the broomstick room.

"Now quickly!" said Hop. "Jump on whilst those two up there are fighting. They've forgotten all about us!"

The mermaid jumped on. Skip jumped on, and so did Hop—but oh dear, there wasn't any room for Jump! The broomstick only held three!

"It'll break if we have four!" groaned Hop. "Now what are we to do!"

"Leave me behind, of course!" said the mermaid, and jumped off again.

"Certainly *not*!" said all the brownies at once, and pulled her on again.

Then Jump made a brave speech.

"I'm not coming," he said. "It was my fault that we came to this island. I wanted to see what was on it. So I'm going to be the one to stay behind."

Well, there was no time to be lost in arguing, so poor Jump *was* left behind.

> "Onaby O,
> Away we'll go,
> Onaby Eye
> Up in the sky!"

said Hop. And off went the broomstick out of the window, while Jump stood on the ground, and watched them fly away from him up into the moonlit sky.

Their Adventure in the Land of Giants

THE broomstick went sailing away in the air, and Hop, Skip, and the mermaid clung to it tightly. They were all very sad, thinking of poor Jump left behind. They didn't know *what* might happen to him.

"Poor Jump," said the mermaid.

"Poor, poor Jump," said Skip.

"Poor, poor, poor——" began Hop—then he stopped.

"I say!" he said hopefully.

"What?" asked the other two.

"Supposing I rub some of the ointment that makes people bigger on to the broomstick! It might make it grow bigger!"

"Then we could go back and fetch Jump!" cried the mermaid.

So Hop got out the yellow ointment and rubbed some of it on to the end of the broomstick.

It immediately grew much smaller, and Hop nearly fell off! He just managed to hang on round Skip's waist.

"Oh, you silly!" cried Skip, "that's the wrong ointment."

Quickly he took the purple ointment from Hop's pocket, though he nearly tumbled off in reaching it.

Immediately it grew enormously large.

"Gracious!" giggled Hop, who was now sitting down firmly again, "there's room for twenty people at least!"

They turned the broomstick back to the island, and soon after arrived at the castle again. They landed at the front door.

There was a terrible noise going on, and dust flew in clouds out of the windows of one of the upstairs rooms.

"They're still trying to settle who's the strongest!" said Hop. "I'll run and fetch Jump!"

He jumped off and ran indoors. There he found Jump, looking very scared indeed. How astonished and glad he was to see Hop!

"Come on, you brave little brownie!" called Hop. "We've made the broomstick bigger, and there's room for you!"

Jump scurried out with Hop, and mounted the broomstick with the others. Then once more the magic rhyme was said, and the broomstick rose into the air.

"Oh, I *am* glad to be with you!" said Jump, sighing gladly. "The wizard and the red goblin were behaving in a terrible manner. They kept changing each other into different things, and chasing about all over the place!"

"Well, they're both about as strong as each other!" said Hop cheerfully; "so they'll probably have a jolly time fighting each other for a good many days yet!"

The broomstick went sailing on and on over the sea in the bright moonlight, and soon left the island far behind.

Suddenly the mermaid gave a shriek of joy.

"There is my home!" she cried. "There is my home!"

The brownies looked down, and saw two or three brown rocks sticking up out of the sea. On them lay mermaids and mermen.

"Quick! Turn the broom downwards!" cried the mermaid. Jump turned it, and soon they were gaily gliding down to the rocks.

Splash! splash! All the mermaids and mermen slid into the water and disappeared when they saw the broomstick gliding down to them.

Bump! It came to rest on one of the rocks.

"Come back! Come back!" called the mermaid. "It's the little mermaid Golden-hair come back! I've been rescued!"

Up popped all the mermen and mermaids again,

and directly they saw that it *really* was Golden-hair, *what* a fuss they made! They cried over her and laughed over her, and patted her and kissed her.

Then one of the mermen brought a shell full of sea-water, and said a spell over it. Golden-hair put her goblin feet into it, and to the brownies' astonishment they changed into a beautiful glittering tail.

Then, flick! Golden-hair slipped into the water, and swam about joyfully with the others.

"Stay with us!" she cried. "We will give you a lovely time!"

"No, thank you," answered Hop. "We'd very much like to, but we are in search of a stolen Princess, so we must go."

The brownies hopped on to the broomstick again, waved good-bye to the merfolk, sang the magic rhyme, and were soon off again.

"I'm glad we were able to rescue Golden-hair," said Jump. "I do wonder where we'll go to next!"

"We mustn't any of us go to sleep," said Hop, "else we'll fall off the broomstick into the sea! Hold on tight till the morning!"

All night long the broom sailed over the sea. Soon the moon went down, and the brownies grew very sleepy indeed.

As the sun rose, they saw that they had left the sea behind at last, and were flying over a wooded country.

"Let's go down here," said Hop, yawning. "I'm longing to go to sleep."

So they turned the broom downwards, and were soon among the trees.

"What enormous trees!" exclaimed Skip in astonishment. "I've never seen such big ones before."

They *were* enormous. When the brownies had landed safely on the ground they craned their necks backwards to try to see the tops of the trees —but they couldn't.

"And just look at the grass!" cried Hop. "It's as tall as a house! And, goodness me, is this a buttercup? Why, I could easily go to sleep in one of the buds!"

"I could go to sleep *anywhere*!" yawned Jump, lying down on a daisy-leaf that was as big as a bed. "Good night, everybody!"

"Well, we'll explore the country when we wake," said Hop, and he chose a leaf too. Skip climbed into a bud and very soon all the brownies were fast asleep.

Suddenly they were awakened by an enormous noise.

Crash, crash, crash, crash!

Hop woke up with a jump, and looked round him. To his amazement he saw walking by him the biggest pair of boots he had ever seen. They seemed as large as two small trees. Hop looked above them.

"Gracious!" he said, "there's legs in the boots!"

The brownies looked above the legs, and then, with a shout of fear, saw that the legs belonged to a body, and that the body had an enormous head with eyes like little lakes.

"Ow!" cried Hop, "it's a giant! We've come to Giantland!"

"Quick!" said Skip. "Hide before he sees us!"

But it was too late. The giant had seen them, and was staring at them in just as much astonishment as they had stared at him. Before they could run and hide, a great hand had come down and picked them all up. Then they were swished up into the air near the giant's head, whilst he had a good look at them.

"Brownies!" said the giant, in a voice like very near thunder. "Brownies! Oh, the tiny wee things!"

"Let us go!" yelled Hop in his loudest voice.

"Oh, he squeaks like a mouse!" said the giant, with a smile that showed enormous white teeth. "Squeak again, little man!"

"I'm not squeaking!" shouted Hop angrily. "I'm shouting at you. Put me down, you're squashing me to bits."

"Squeak away, squeak away," said the giant. "I'll take you home and show you to my wife. What a find!"

He stuffed the three brownies into his coat pocket and strode off.

"Oh, it's like riding inside a camel's hump!" said Hop, as the giant's coat flapped in the wind, and swayed to and fro as he walked.

"What a terrible fix we're in *now*!" groaned Skip. "How in the world can we get away from here?"

The brownies clung together as frightened as could be. At last the giant stopped, put his hand in his pocket, and pulled out the three brownies.

"Look, wife!" he said in his booming voice. "What do you think of *these* little chaps?"

"Oh!" thundered his wife in delight. "Are they real?"

"Real enough!" said the giant, setting them down on a table as big as a field. "Now then, squeak!" he said, and gave Hop such a poke with his finger that he fell over and nearly tumbled off the table.

The giant's wife was delighted with them.

"We'll give a tea-party this afternoon, and show them to all our friends," she said.

"No, no, let us go back and find our broom-stick!" begged Skip.

"Hark at him squeaking!" cried the giant in delight, and gave him a poke that sent him head over heels.

The giant's wife carefully put them into a box with some holes punched in to let the air through. She also put in a thimbleful of water and some crumbs of bread. The thimble was as big as a barrel and the crumbs as big as loaves, so that the brownies had more than enough to eat and drink.

They were very upset indeed.

"We seem to do nothing but get caught by someone or other," groaned Hop. "If only we could go back to Fairyland!"

61

"Well, goodness knows what's going to happen to us *this* time!" said Skip gloomily. "We're so small, luckily, compared with the giants, that they probably won't eat us! We shouldn't make more than a mouthful!"

"Ugh! don't be horrid!" said Jump, who didn't like the conversation at all. "Let's talk of something cheerful."

All the day the giant's wife kept taking off the lid, and peeping in at the brownies to see if they were all right. She put in three lumps of sugar for them to sit down on, and was very much amused to see them perched up on them. They heard her big voice rumbling all day long. The clatter that her pots and pans made sounded like crashes of thunder.

When the afternoon came the giant's wife took off the lid of the box and lifted the brownies out on to the table. She put some fresh water in the thimble, and gave them a rag as big as a table-cloth for a towel, and told them to wash themselves and make themselves smart.

"My guests will soon be here," she boomed, "and I want you to be a surprise for them."

When the brownies had washed themselves and smoothed back their hair the giant's wife picked them all up and carried them into another room, where a table was laid for tea. In the middle was a cake and on top, made of pink icing, were three little chairs!

"Buttons and buttercups!" groaned Hop. "Look what she's done! We've got to sit on the cake!"

Sure enough they had. The giantess popped each one, bump! on to a chair.

"Now you sit there and don't move an eyelash," she said. "Everyone will think you're dolls. When I say, 'Now I'll cut the cake,' you're to jump out of your chairs and cheer!"

The brownies felt very much annoyed. They didn't like the idea of pretending to be dolls at all, just to amuse a lot of giants.

Skip jumped off his chair crossly.

"No!" he shouted loudly, "I won't!"

The giantess picked him up and gave him such a squeeze that he felt he was going to choke.

"Now you do as you're told," she scolded, in her enormous voice, "or I'll give you to the fowls to peck!"

Skip sat down very quickly on his chair. He didn't like the idea of being given to the fowls at all. Nor did the others. They all sat as still as could be, in case the giantess said anything more.

All around them gleamed great knives and forks, and spoons, and huge glasses that seemed as big as houses. From the kitchen came a very nice smell.

"That makes me feel hungry," said Hop, sighing.

"What about chipping a bit off the cake?" asked Skip. "The giantess has gone out of the room for a minute!"

"Bite the knobs off the backs of your chairs," said Jump. "They're delicious."

The three brownies bit them off, and very delicious they were. They tasted of honey and sugar, and the brownies were just going to nibble pieces off the back of their chairs, too, when a most enormous noise made them fall off their seats in fright.

It was the guests knocking at the front door!

RAT-TAT-TAT!

The brownies began to tremble. It was rather terrifying to have to face a lot of giants at once.

"They're so careless in picking us up and putting us down," groaned Hop.

"And I *hate* being held tight," said Skip.

"Sh!" said Jump, "here they come."

With an enormous noise of tramping, talking, and laughing, in walked six of the largest giants you could imagine. They were followed by the giantess and her husband, both of whom were smaller than their guests.

64

"HA!" said a giant, seating himself at the table, "I'M HUNGRY!"

"Ho," said another, "I'M THIRSTY."

The giantess made haste to bring in the teapot, and soon every giant was stuffing himself with sandwiches as big as mattresses. The noise they made too! It sounded like twenty thousand pigs feeding at once.

Suddenly one of them noticed the cake.

"Ho," he said, "WHAT A FINE CAKE!"

All the giants looked at it, and thought it was very fine indeed.

"I've never seen such nice figures before as those you've got sitting on your cake," said a giant.

"VERY NICE INDEED," bellowed a giant with an extra loud voice.

All this time the brownies hadn't dared to move in case the giantess should keep her word, and throw them to the fowls. They sat like dummies, staring straight in front of them.

"They look quite real," said a giant, and bent closer to look at them. Then he took his fork and was just going to poke Hop with it when that terrified brownie leapt up into the air in fright, and gave an anguished yell.

The giant was so astonished that he dropped his fork with a clatter, and sat open-mouthed. All the giants stared at the brownies in the greatest amazement.

The giantess thought it was time to surprise her guests a little more.

"Now I'll cut the cake," she said.

At once Hop, Skip, and Jump leapt out of their chairs and cheered as they had been told to do.

The giants jumped in astonishment.

"They squeak!" said one.

"They move!" said another.

"They must be alive," said a third.

"They *are*," said the giantess proudly. "They're brownies. What do you think of *that* for a surprise?"

She began cutting the cake, and the brownies jumped down on to the table. Directly the giants heard they were brownies they began talking excitedly all at once, and each giant tried to catch a brownie, so as to have a good look at him.

The brownies dodged their great fingers as best they could. They hid behind glasses and under the edges of the plates, and Hop even jumped into the salt-cellar, and covered himself with salt—but it was no good. They were caught and held, and passed from one giant to another.

They hated it, for the giants held them so tightly, and seemed to enjoy giving them a poke now and again, just to see them roll head over heels.

"I shall break my neck soon," panted Hop. "That's twice I've been poked over."

"Let's pretend we're hurt," said Skip; "perhaps they'll stop then."

So Hop lay down on the table and groaned, Skip walked about with a limp, and Jump held his head as if it hurt him.

The giantess, who had quite a kind heart, was most upset.

"You've hurt the poor little mites," she cried. "Look at them! Leave them alone now, do, or you'll kill them, and I want to keep them for pets, and give them to my children when they come back from their aunt's."

"Oh!" groaned Hop. "Did you hear what she said? Goodness knows what giant children would do with us! What a terrible fix we are in!"

The giantess brought their thimble filled with lemonade, and put some cake crumbs on a cotton-reel.

"Here you are," she said, giving them lumps of sugar to sit on. "Sit down at this cotton-reel table, and have your tea, while we watch you."

The brownies sat down and took the cake crumbs. They were as large as cakes and very nice. When they wanted a drink they went to the thimble and sipped the lemonade.

The giants soon grew tired of watching them, and fell silent. The giantess rose and began clearing away the dishes into the kitchen. Then, one by one, the giants fell asleep.

Hop looked round at them.

SNORE, SNORE, SNORE, went the giants, sleepy after their big meal. They breathed so heavily that they nearly blew the brownies off the table.

"I say," shouted Hop, trying to make himself heard over the snoring, "let's escape!"

"How?" shouted Skip. "If one of the giants wakes whilst we are slipping away he'll wake the others, and they'll all come thundering after us and kill us."

"Think of an idea, Hop," shouted Jump.

Hop thought—then he grinned.

"What about the ointment?" he shouted back. "Shall we use that on the giants whilst they're asleep?"

"Yes, yes!" shrieked Skip and Jump, nearly deafened by the snores of the giants. "Get it out, quick, Hop."

Hop got out the boxes of ointment and opened them.

"There isn't very much left of either of them," he shouted. "We'll use both and see what happens. Here, Skip, take the purple ointment, and

I'll take the yellow. Jump, you keep a watch for the giantess."

Hop and Skip ran across the table, and each climbed up a giant's arm on to his shoulder. They couldn't reach his forehead, so they rubbed the ointment on to his chin, and hoped it would act just as well.

Then down they clambered, and up on to two more giants' shoulders. Hop was nearly blown away by one tremendous giant, who puffed him nearly off his arm.

At last all the sleeping giants had the magic ointment rubbed on to their chins.

"Now listen!" shouted Hop, whose voice was getting quite hoarse. "I'm going to say the magic words. The giants will grow smaller and bigger, and they'll wake up in a terrible fright. We've got to escape whilst they're in a muddle. Climb off the table first."

The brownies clambered down the table-cloth, slid down the table-legs, and landed bump on to the floor. They ran to the door.

Then Hop called out the magic words.

At once three of the giants grew so much smaller that they were only about three times as big as the brownies. The other four grew so much bigger that their heads bumped against the ceiling, their chairs broke with their weight, and they fell on to the floor with yells of fright.

"Oh! Oh! Oh!" they shouted in astonishment. The giantess came running in to see what was the matter. She couldn't believe her eyes.

"What's happened?" she cried. "Oh, what's happened? Why have some of you grown small and some of you big? Oh dear, dear, dear!"

"Come on," said Hop, and he and the other brownies ran out of the door. The giantess saw them.

"Oh, you've worked a spell on them!" she cried angrily. "I'll catch you, you wicked little things."

Hop, Skip, and Jump raced across the kitchen floor as hard as they could, and out into the garden. They hid under a large leaf and watched the huge feet of the giantess go clomping by in search of them.

"Good thing she didn't tread on us," said Hop. Then he saw something that made him shiver in fright.

"Look!" he said. "There's a giant hen—and there's another one—they're scratching in the ground. Oh my, we've run into the fowl yard!"

The brownies trembled in fear. The hens came nearer and nearer, clucking and squawking as they scratched for grain.

Suddenly one of them saw Hop under the big leaf. She pecked at him. He jumped away only just in time.

"Run!" he cried. "It's the only chance we have!"

They ran from beneath the leaf and tore across the yard.

"Squawk—squawk!" cried all the hens, and tore after them.

"They'll catch us!" panted Jump.

Suddenly Hop saw a large hole in front of him. Quick as lightning he jumped into it and pulled the others after him.

"It's a worm-hole!" he gasped. "Come on, it's our only chance of escaping those horrid birds."

The hens were pecking and scraping around the hole, their beaks sounding like picks and hammers.

But once more the brownies were safe, for the worm-hole was like a narrow tunnel, and they could pass along it easily, one after another.

"I hope we don't meet a worm," said Skip, "it would be rather awkward, wouldn't it?"

"I'd much rather meet a worm than a crowd of huge giants, or a pack of greedy birds," said Hop cheerfully. "Come on! Goodness knows where this tunnel leads to, but anyway, it must lead *somewhere*!"

Their Adventure in the Land of Clever People

THE three brownies went on through the dark tunnel, hoping they would soon find it came to an end. It felt rather sticky, and Hop said it must be because a worm had lately passed along it.

Just as he said that the brownies heard a peculiar noise. "Oh my! I do believe it's a worm coming!" Hop groaned.

It *was* a worm, a simply enormous one, for its body filled up the whole tunnel.

"Ho," shouted Hop in a panic, "don't come any farther, Mr. Worm; you'll squash us to bits!"

The worm stopped wriggling in surprise.

"What are you doing in my tunnel?" he asked.

"Nothing much," said Skip. "Just escaping from a lot of greedy birds!"

"Oh!" said the worm with a shudder. "I know all about birds. I've had my tail pecked off twice by the greedy things."

"Do you know where this tunnel leads to?" asked Jump.

"It leads to all sorts of places," said the worm. "You'll find cross-roads a little farther on, and a sign-post."

"Oh, thanks," said Jump. "Then I think we'll be getting on."

"So will I," said the worm, and began to wriggle towards the brownies.

"Stop!" they shouted. "There isn't room for you to go past us!"

"But I *must*," said the worm. "I've an appointment with my tailor at six o'clock. He's making me a few more rings for my body."

"Oh, *do* go backwards till you get to the crossroads," begged Hop.

"I'm going backwards *now*," said the worm. "At least I think I am. It's so muddling being able to use both your ends, you know. I never know which way I'm *really* going."

"It must be *very* muddling," said Skip. "But please don't push past us; you're rather sticky, you know, and you'll spoil our suits, and *we* haven't got a tailor like you!"

"Dear, dear, you ought to have," said the worm. "I'll tell you what I'll do. I'll bore you a little tunnel to stand in whilst I go past; then I shan't spoil your suits."

The worm began to make them a little passage leading out of the main tunnel.

"There you are," he said; "get in there, and you'll be quite safe."

The brownies hopped in. Then, rustle-squelch-rustle! The worm pulled his long body past them, called good-bye, and left them.

"Well, thank goodness, we've got over *that* difficulty," said Hop. "Now let's get to the cross-roads before we meet any other worms."

On they went again, meeting no one but a centipede, who fled past in such a hurry on his many legs that the brownies didn't know *what* he was.

"Must be the fast train to Wormland, I should think!" said Hop, picking himself up, for the centipede had rushed straight between his legs.

Soon the brownies saw a light in the distance. They hurried towards it, and found that they stood at the cross-roads. In the middle was a sign-post with a lamp on top.

"To Giantland," Hop read. "Ugh! That's the way we've just come. What's this other way? To the Land of Giggles! That sounds silly. To Cross-patch Country! *That* won't do for us. Now what's this last one?"

All the brownies peered at it.

"To the Land of Clever People," they read.

"Clever People *might* be able to tell us the way to Witchland," said Hop.

"Yes, let's go," said Jump.

"I hope they'll let us in," said Skip doubtfully.

"I don't really feel very clever, you know."

"You're not," said Hop. "*I'm* the clever one."

"Yes, you were clever enough to get us all sent out of Fairyland," grumbled Skip.

"Don't let's quarrel," said Hop. "Come on, and see what this new land is like."

Off they went again, and found that the tunnel they were now in sloped upwards, and was lighted by many little green lamps.

"Green for safety, anyway," said Jump cheerfully.

The lamps suddenly turned red. The brownies jumped in fright.

"Red for danger!" said Skip in a shaky voice.

The lamps turned blue. Hop thought of an idea.

"I expect it's somebody in the Land of Clever People, showing us how clever they are," he whispered. Then aloud he said in an admiring voice, "H'm, blue for cleverness!"

All the lamps turned back to green.

"There you are!" whispered Hop. "Green for safety again."

They went on up the slope, and came to a corner. Just round the bend was a turnstile, and at it was seated an ugly little man, with an enormous bald head. He wore spectacles, and was writing in a huge book. As the brownies drew near he looked at them over his spectacles. Then he spoke in a way that gave the brownies rather a surprise:

> "Good morning. Do I understand,
>   You wish to enter in this Land?"

"He's talking in poetry!" said Jump. "Isn't he clever! Are we supposed to answer in poetry too?"

"We can't," said Skip. "So that settles it."

He turned to the turnstile man.

"Yes, we want to come in," he said. "You see we . . ."

The bald-headed man interrupted him:

> "Please talk in rhyme. Unless you do,
>   I simply cannot let you through."

"Oh goodness gracious!" groaned the brownies.

"They must be *terribly* clever people," said Hop. "Let's see if we can't make up an answer in rhyme."

They thought for some time, and at last they found one they thought would do. Hop went up to the turnstile man and bowed.

> "Will you kindly let us through,
>   There's lots of things we want to do,"

he said. At once the man waved his hand to tell them to pass, and his turnstile clicked as they went through. Before they left him he handed them a book of rules.

"Keep every rule that's written here,
    You'll find them printed nice and clear,"
he said in his singsong voice.

"Thank you very much indeed,
    I like to have a book to read,"
answered Hop, as easily as anything.

"Hop!" cried Jump, when they had got out of the turnstile man's hearing. "Hop! That *was* clever of you! How *did* you think of it?"

"It just came into my head," said Hop, quite as surprised as the others. "I believe I'll be quite good at it."

"What does the book of rules say?" asked Jump. Hop read it, and told the others.

"Nothing much," he said. "Always talk in

77

rhyme. Make up a new riddle every day. Answer one. Not much, is it?"

"I don't know," said Skip doubtfully. "I think making up riddles is very hard."

"What happens if we can't make up riddles or answer them?" asked Jump.

"I'll look and see," said Hop, turning over the page. "Oh, buttons and buttercups!"

"What, Hop?" asked Skip and Jump.

"Anyone who can't make up riddles or answer them is spanked for being stupid," said Hop in dismay.

"Oh, I *do* wish we hadn't come here!" said Jump. "This is *your* fault again, Hop. You're always leading us into trouble."

"Let's go back to the turnstile man, and ask him to let us out," said Hop.

So they went back.

"Please let us out again, because,
      We find we cannot keep your laws,"
said Hop, after scratching his head and thinking hard for five minutes.

The bald-headed man shook his head.

"Find rule number thirty-two,
      And that will tell you what to do,"
he told them.

Hop found it and read it.

"We can't get out of the Land of Clever People until we think of something that their Very Wise Man cannot do," he told the others sadly. "There isn't much hope for *us*, then."

"Stay here all our lives, I suppose," said Skip gloomily.

"And be spanked every day," said Jump, still more gloomily.

The three brownies went sadly up the tunnel. They hadn't gone very far before they saw daylight, and to their joy they found that they were once more above ground. They ran out of the tunnel, and danced about in the sunlight. Then they stopped and looked to see what sort of country they were in.

"My!" said Hop. "It's rather queer, isn't it? It all looks so proper!"

It certainly *did* look proper. The houses were set down in perfectly straight lines. All the windows were the same size, and all the doors. All the knockers were the same, and they all shone brightly.

The people looked very proper too. They all wore spectacles, and had very large heads, and all the men were bald. If everybody hadn't been rather short and tubby, they would have looked frightening, but as it was they looked rather funny.

Skip began to giggle.

"They don't look as if they ever smiled!" he chuckled.

A fat little policeman came up to them. He put his hand heavily on Skip's shoulder.

"You mustn't giggle here, you know,
Or else to prison you must go.
This is not the Land of Giggles——"

He stopped and looked at the brownies. The brownies looked back. Evidently he expected them to finish the rhyme.

"Oh dear!" thought Hop. "Whatever will make a rhyme for giggles? What an awful word!"

The policeman coughed and repeated his lines again. Then he took out his note-book.

Hop began to tremble.

"This is not the Land of Giggles," said the policeman in an awful, this-is-the-last-time sort of voice.

"How your little finger wiggles!" said Hop suddenly.

The policeman looked at his little finger in surprise. It wasn't wiggling. Still Hop had made a rhyme, so he closed up his notebook and marched solemnly off.

"That was a narrow escape," said Hop in a whisper. "It's a mean trick to leave someone to finish what you're saying, in rhyme. Now, remember, for goodness' sake don't giggle. We don't want to be sent to prison, or to the Land of Giggles, do we?"

Night was falling. Lamps began to shine in the little streets.

"We'd better find a place to sleep," said Skip, with a yawn. Another policeman suddenly appeared behind them. Hop saw him in time, and made a rhyme hastily, to fit his last sentence.

"Oh, look at that excited sheep!" he said, pointing behind him.

There was no sheep, of course, and by the time the policeman had discovered that, the brownies had fled down the street.

They came to the neatest little house imaginable. In the window was a card. On it was printed:

STEP INSIDE AND YOU WILL SEE
LODGINGS HERE FOR TWO OR THREE.

"*Just* the thing," said Hop. "Let us ring," he added hastily, as another policeman came round the corner and looked at them.

He rang. The door opened, and a kind-faced old woman looked out.

"Would you let us stay with you?" he asked, hoping that the old woman would finish the rhyme.

"What can you pay me if you do?" asked she, at once.

"Would sixpence be enough to pay?" said Hop.

"Oh, yes, it would. Please come this way," said the old woman, and led them inside.

The house was very neat inside. The room the old woman took them to was queer-looking. It had knobs here and there on the wall, and Hop longed to pull them and see what happened.

"This is where you are to sleep," said their guide, and waited for Hop to finish the rhyme.

"Always look before you leap," said Hop solemnly. The woman stared at him and went out.

"This rhyming business is making me tired," said Hop, when the door closed. "I do hope we find some way of getting out of this land soon. What about pressing a few of these knobs? Look, this one's marked SOUP."

He pressed it. A little door flew open in the wall, and there stood three mugs of steaming soup!

"Goodness!" said Skip, "*that's* clever, if you like. Let's have the soup!"

They soon finished it up, and began pressing more knobs. The one marked CHOCOLATE brought them three packets of chocolates, and the one marked APPLES a dish of apples. They thought it a very good idea.

"Now, if these Clever People had ideas like this *only*," said Hop, "and no silly nonsense about rhymes and riddles and things, this would be a pleasant place to live in."

He pressed a knob marked BED. Immediately a bed rose from the floor under them, and stood there ready to be slept in. The brownies rose with it, and found themselves sitting on it.

Skip gave a loud giggle.

At once the window flew up.

"Was that a giggle that I heard?" demanded a policeman, peering into the room.

"No, just a cough. Don't be absurd," shouted Hop. The window shut with a bang.

"There are policemen everywhere here," whispered Hop. "For goodness' sake don't giggle any more, and only talk in whispers."

At that moment there came a knock on their door. It opened, and in came a bright-eyed, gaily-dressed little girl.

"Hallo," she said. "I heard one of you laughing. Are you from the Land of Giggles, by any chance?"

"No, we're not," said Hop in astonishment. "Why aren't you talking in rhyme?"

"I'm not one of the Clever People," said the little girl. "I can't make up rhymes properly, so I usually don't talk at all. I come from the Land of Giggles."

"What are you here for, then?" asked Skip.

The little girl hung her head.

"I was discontented in my own land," she said, "and I thought I was too clever for my people. So I came here, and now I can't get away, because I can't think of anything that the Very Wise Man can't do. And I get spanked every single day because I can't make up riddles or answer them."

"Who asks them?" asked Hop.

"Oh, everybody goes to the market-place and stands in a row for their examination each morning," explained the little girl. "Then the Very Wise Man comes along, and you have to ask him your riddle and answer his. If you don't, he sends you to be spanked. It's to teach you to be clever."

"I don't think it's clever to do *that* sort of thing," said Skip, feeling sure he would be spanked every day that came.

"If you can help me to get back to my own people, I'd be so grateful," said the little girl, nodding her brown curls.

"We'll help you," said Hop, wondering however they could.

When the little girl had gone the brownies jumped into bed and were soon fast asleep.

Their Adventure in the Land of Clever People
(continued)

WHEN morning came the brownies woke up very hungry. They pressed a few knobs and got a simply lovely breakfast of porridge, honey, and cocoa.

"Now we'd better think of some riddles," said Hop. "All be quiet and think hard."

So they thought hard. Hop thought of one first.

"What pillar is never used in building?" he asked.

"Don't know," said the others.

"Why, a *cater*pillar, of course," said Hop, with a chuckle.

"Very good indeed!" said Skip. "Listen, I've got one now. What walks on its head all day?"

"Tell us!" said the others.

"The nail in your shoes!" chuckled Skip. "Now, Jump!"

"What lion is loose in the fields?" asked Jump.

"I know!" cried Hop: "the *dande*lion!"

"Right!" said Jump. "Listen, what's that?"

It was a bell ringing.

"It must be to call us to the market-place," said Hop. "Come on."

They all raced outside, and saw a great stream of solemn, fat little people going down the street. The brownies joined them, and soon came to a wide market-place. The people ranged themselves in straight rows. A clock struck nine.

Trumpets blew, and down the steps of the Town Hall came the Very Wise Man. He had bigger spectacles than anyone else, and a very, *very* big head.

Then began the examination. First the Very Wise Man asked his riddle, and then a Clever Person answered it and asked his.

On went the Very Wise Man to the next person. "Everybody answers all right," whispered Hop. "No one's getting spanked."

Just then the Very Wise Man came to the little girl who had spoken to the brownies the night before. She couldn't answer her riddle, and she was sent off to be spanked by the Spanker, who lived in a little house near by.

Then came the brownies' turn.

"What pillar is never used in building?" asked Hop, rather shaky at the knees.

"Pooh—a caterpillar!" said the Very Wise Man.

"What walks on its head all day?" asked Skip nervously.

"Pooh—nail in your shoe," said the Very Wise Man.

"Er-er—what lion is loose in the fields?" asked Jump, almost forgetting his riddle, when he felt the Very Wise Man's eyes on him.

"Pooh—a dandelion," said the Very Wise Man. "Very feeble. Now answer me this—Why is a toasting-fork?"

"Why is a toasting-fork?" said Hop, puzzled. "It doesn't make sense, does it?"

"Off to the Spanker's!" roared the Very Wise Man. Poor Hop went off to join the little girl.

"Now *you*," said the Very Wise Man to Skip. "Why is a garden-rake?"

"But *that* doesn't make sense either," said Skip. "It isn't a proper riddle."

"Off to the Spanker's," roared the Very Wise Man again. He turned to Jump.

"Why is a porcupine?" he asked.

"*I* don't know," said Jump.

"Off to the Spanker's!" shouted the Very Wise Man, and went on asking the Clever People more riddles which they seemed to answer perfectly.

The brownies were well spanked by the Spanker, who was a solemn little man with soft eyes and a hard hand.

They were very angry about it.

"It's all nonsense," said Hop crossly. "He didn't ask fair riddles. I'll jolly well ask him to do something he can't do, and then we'll get away from here."

"Well, if you can do that," said the little girl, drying her tears, "don't forget to take me with you."

All that day the brownies wandered about the Land of Clever People with the little girl. It was a very solemn, proper land, and nobody laughed or skipped or ran.

Poor Skip and Jump were sent to the Spanker twice for not making a rhyme when they spoke. They felt sorrier than ever that they had left Fairyland. Little tubby policemen seemed to be everywhere, and they soon began to feel that it was dangerous even to whisper.

Next morning they couldn't think of any riddles, nor answer any, so off they went to be spanked again. Hop was getting very tired of it.

"I'll go and ask the Very Wise Man to do something he can't do," he said. "Where do I go?" he asked the little girl.

"Go to the Town Hall at three o'clock in the afternoon," she said. "You'll find him there, waiting."

So off the brownies went. They marched up the

steps and found the Very Wise Man sitting in a
great red chair, studying an old, old book.

"Good afternoon, O Very Wise Man,
    Do what I ask you, if you can,"
began Hop.

"Build a castle in half an hour,
    With an entrance gate and one big tower."

The Very Wise Man descended from his throne
and walked out of the hall. He drew a wide circle
in the market-place, muttered a few words, and
waved his arms.

Immediately there sounded the noise of hammering and clattering, although nothing could be seen.

But lo and behold! At the end of half an hour, there stood in front of the astonished brownies a wonderful castle with an entrance gate and one big gleaming tower!

Hop, Skip, and Jump were too amazed to say a word. Then, with a wave of his hand, the Very Wise Man caused the castle to vanish completely. After that he turned to Hop.

"Off to the Spanker's," he said.

So off Hop had to go.

"I'll think of something much more difficult *next* time," he decided.

For days Hop and the others tried to think of new riddles, and to puzzle out something difficult to ask the Very Wise Man to do. It didn't seem any good at all. They always seemed to be either going to or coming back from the Spanker's.

At three o'clock each day the brownies always went to the Town Hall with something new and difficult to ask the Very Wise Man to perform, hoping that he wouldn't be able to do it.

Once they asked him if he could make a ladder that reached to the stars, and he made a lovely one out of a rainbow. Hop wanted to climb it, but the Very Wise Man wouldn't let him.

"You might escape and that would be
   A most annoying thing for me,"
he said.

Another afternoon the brownies asked him to
make a cloak which, when he put it on, would
make him invisible. He did it at once, popped on
the cloak, and none of the brownies could see
where he was. He had disappeared!

"Let us put it on as well,
   And try the lovely magic spell,"
begged Hop, who thought that if only he could
throw the cloak around himself, and the other two,
he might be able to escape unseen.

But the Very Wise Man wouldn't let him. He
sent them all off to the Spanker's instead.

One evening the brownies were feeling very
miserable indeed.

"I believe we shall have to stay here for ever,"
groaned Hop.

"So shall I," sighed the little girl, rumpling her
curly head in despair.

"Don't rumple your hair like that," said Skip,
"or you'll be sent for a spanking again."

He smoothed down her hair for her, and then
picked up a curly bit that had broken off.

"Isn't it curly?" he said. "I wonder if I can
make it straight."

He pulled it out straight—but it went back curly. He wetted it—but it was still curly. Then he gave it to the others, and *they* tried to make it straight. But they couldn't.

"The Very Wise Man could make it straight in half a minute," said Hop mournfully.

"Well, I should like to see him do it," said Skip. "It simply *won't* go straight."

"Let's ask him to-morrow!" said Jump hopefully.

So next day the three brownies and the little girl went to the Town Hall at three o'clock. The Very Wise Man was there as usual.

"Your next request I now await,"
said he, leaving Hop to finish the rhyme. But Hop was ready, for once.

"Then make this curly hair quite straight!"
said Hop, handing it to him.

The Very Wise Man took it, and looked scornful to think he had such an easy task.

He pulled it out straight, then let it go one end. The hair sprang back into curl again.

He wetted it, and pulled it straight once more. It sprang back curlier than ever!

He stamped on it. He clapped it between his hands. He waved it in the air. He put it between the pages of a book.

Not a bit of good did anything do! It only made the hair twice as curly as before!

Then the Very Wise Man called for a hot iron and a cold iron. He ironed it first with one and then with the other.

But the hair sprang back to its curliness, and *wouldn't* stay straight.

The brownies watched in the greatest excitement, their hearts beating quickly.

"I don't believe he can do it!" cried Jump.

The Very Wise Man was so worried that he didn't notice Jump hadn't spoken in rhyme. He couldn't think *what* to do with that wretched hair.

At last he knew he was beaten. He sank back on his throne, mopped his forehead, and asked Hop to let him off.

"Yes, I will," said Hop, "if you will do what I want you to do. If not, I'll tell all the Clever People how stupid you are."

"Talk in rhyme,
All the time,"

said the Very Wise Man.

"Nonsense!" said Hop. "I'm not going to talk in rhyme any more. It's silly when you can talk better another way. Now, are you going to do what I want?"

"Yes," said the Very Wise Man sadly.

"First of all," said Hop, "tell me where the Princess Peronel is."

"In Witchland with Witch Green-eyes," answered the Very Wise Man.

"How can we get there?" asked Hop.

"Take the Green Railway to Fiddlestick Field," said the Very Wise Man, "and ask the Saucepan Man to tell you the way. He knows it."

"Now the next thing is," said Hop, feeling he was doing very well, "you must let this little girl go back to the Land of Giggles."

"Oh no, I can't do that," said the Very Wise Man crossly.

"All right," said Hop, "I'm going out to tell the people all about how you couldn't make a curly hair straight."

"Oh, you *are* brave, Hop!" cried the little girl, kissing him. "Thank you for sticking up for me."

Hop caught hold of the Very Wise Man's shoulder, and daringly shook him.

"Will you let her go?" he demanded.

"Yes, yes! Leave me alone!" growled the Very Wise Man.

"And the next thing is, take us out of this horrid land of yours," said Hop. "You're not Clever People a bit, you only think you are. You think it's clever to be solemn and proper and never laugh or skip. Well, it isn't. It's just silly."

"Come along," said the Very Wise Man, suddenly. "I'll take you out of the land now. I shall be glad to be rid of you."

He strode down the hall, out into the market-place and through the streets of the town. The brownies and the little girl followed him in delight.

At last they came to a high wall, and in it was a gateway and a turnstile. A big-headed, fat little man sat there. He stared at them in surprise.

"Am I to let these people out?" he asked doubtfully.

"Yes, you are," cried Hop, laughing to see the little man's horror when he heard him speak without rhyming.

Then Hop turned to the Very Wise Man.

"There's just one thing more you've to do," he said.

"I will do it," said the Very Wise Man.

"Well, listen," said Hop. "Answer me some of the silly riddles you asked us each morning—Now, why is a toasting-fork? Why is a garden-rake? Why is a porcupine?"

The Very Wise Man hung his head.

"I don't know," he said.

"Well, if you aren't mean and horrid!" cried

Hop. "It's unfair to ask people riddles you know haven't got answers, and then send them to be spanked because they don't answer them. Now I'll give you just one more chance—Why is a garden-rake?"

The Very Wise Man shook his head.

"All right," said Hop, grinning. "Off to the Spanker's with you! Tell him to give you his best spanking!"

The Very Wise Man gave an awful yell and ran away before Hop could say anything more. Hop and the others clicked through the turnstile and chuckled.

"That just serves him right!" said Skip. "He won't be so keen on spanking now!"

Their Adventure on the Green Railway

The brownies looked around. They were in a bare, open country, with the walls of the Land of the Clever People behind them.

"We'd better see you safely back to your country first," said Hop to the little girl, who was dancing about and clapping her hands for joy at having escaped.

"Oh, we'll all travel on the Green Railway," said the little girl. "I'll get out at Giggleswick—that's my station—and you can go on to Fiddlestick Field, if you like, or come and stay with me at my home."

"I think we'd better not do that," said Hop who was beginning to feel that it was far easier to get *into* a strange land than *out* of it. "We might not giggle enough."

"Besides, we want to find out the way to Witchland as soon as we can," said Skip, "so that we can rescue poor little Princess Peronel."

"Well, first of all, where's the Green Railway?" asked Jump.

"Oh, it runs beneath the ground just here," explained the little girl. "I'll show you how to get to it. Look for a big yellow mushroom, all of you."

The brownies began hunting all around.

"I've found a beauty!" cried Hop.

"So have I!" called Skip.

"So have we," said the little girl, running up with Jump. "Bring them here and set them down in a circle."

They all brought their mushrooms. They were very big ones, quite as large as stools, and the brownies were able to stand them up straight, and then sit on the tops.

"Hold tight to your mushrooms," said the little girl, "while I say a magic rhyme."

The brownies held tight.

"Mushrooms, take us down below;
One, two, three, and off we go.
Rikky, tikky, tolly vo!"

cried the little girl.

Whizz-whizz-whizz! The mushrooms suddenly sank down through the ground at a terrific pace. The brownies gasped for breath and held on as tightly as ever they could.

Then bump—bump—bump—bump—the four mushrooms all came to a sudden stop and tipped the brownies off their seats. They rolled on the ground.

"Ha, ha!" laughed the little girl, who was still

sitting on her mushroom. "Anyone can see you're not used to riding mushrooms. Come along, and we'll see if a train is due now."

The brownies picked themselves up and followed the little girl, who was scampering through a cave lighted by one star-shaped lamp.

When she came to the end of it she stopped, and the brownies saw a little door let into the wall. It opened, and the little girl ran through it. The brownies followed her and, to their astonishment, found themselves on a tiny little platform.

A solemn grey rabbit sat there with piles of tickets in front of him.

"One to Giggleswick and three to Fiddlestick Field," said the little girl.

"One penny each," said the grey rabbit, handing out the four tickets. "Next train in five minutes."

Sure enough, in five minutes there came the rattle and clank of a train, and the funniest wee engine ran into the station, dragging behind it a long row of higgledy-piggledy carriages. They had no roof and no seats—only just cushions on the floor.

It was a very crowded train. One carriage was full of velvety moles, who smoked long pipes and talked about the best way to catch beetles. Another carriage was full of giggling people, who seemed to be making jokes and laughing at them as fast as they could.

"Oh, there's some of my own people!" cried the little girl gladly. "They're going to Giggleswick, I expect. Let's get in with them."

So they all jumped in with the laughing people, though the brownies would really rather have got into an empty carriage.

The train went off when the guard waved his flag and blew his whistle. It ran clanking through dark tunnels, and big and little caves. The brownies were very much interested in all they saw and would have liked to talk about it—but the other people in the carriage were so talkative, and laughed so often, that they couldn't get a word in.

The little girl was very much excited; she laughed more than anyone, and told all about her adventures in the Land of Clever People. Hop thought she was nicer *in* that land than out of it, because she didn't giggle so much then.

The train stopped again.

"Burrow Corner!" shouted a sandy rabbit-porter.

The moles all got out, and so did the grey bunnies. Then the train went gaily off again.

The next station was Giggleswick. All the Gigglers got out. The little girl flung her arms

round each of the brownies and hugged them.

"Do, do, *do* come and stay in my country," she begged. "Jump out now, do! We're very merry, and laugh all day!"

"No, we really mustn't," said Hop, who didn't want to go with the Gigglers in the least. "Goodbye, and we're *so* glad you're safe home again."

The train rattled off, and the brownies waved good-bye.

"Well!" said Jump, sitting down on his cushion. "I think I'd rather have to speak in rhyme all day than giggle every minute. What a terrible country to live in!"

"Thank goodness we didn't go there!" said

Hop. "What a lot of queer lands there are outside Fairyland! How I wish we could go back to dear old Brownie Town again!"

"So do I," said Skip, with a sigh. "But I don't expect we'll ever be able to do that, because we shall never be able to find our goodnesses, as the King said we must."

"Oh look!" said Jump, "we're coming out into the open air again!"

The train puffed out of the half-darkness and came to a sunny field. It ran along beside a hedge for some way, and then out on a roadway. All sorts of queer folk were walking there, and all kinds of animals, who looked as if they had been out marketing.

The train stopped whenever anybody hailed it, and lots of people got in.

"We shall never get to Fiddlestick Field," said Hop, when the train stopped for the fifteenth time. "Really, people are treating this train more like a bus! Oh dear, what's happened now?"

The train stopped again. The driver was having a long talk with a friend he had met. The brownies got very impatient.

At last Hop got out and went up to the driver.

"Aren't we ever going on again?" he asked. "We're in a hurry."

"Oh, are you?" said the driver. "Well, I'm going to have tea with my friend here, so you'd better get out and walk. This train won't start till six o'clock."

So saying, the driver jumped from the train, linked his arm in his friend's and strolled off.

All the passengers yawned, settled themselves on their cushions, and went to sleep. The three brownies were very cross.

"Fine sort of train this!" grumbled Skip. "Goodness knows when we'll get to Fiddlestick Field!"

"I've a jolly good mind to drive the train myself," said Hop.

"Oh, Hop, *do*!" cried Jump. "I'm sure you could. Then we could get to Fiddlestick Field tonight."

Hop looked at the engine. It really didn't look very difficult to drive, and he had always longed to be an engine-driver. This seemed a lovely chance.

"All right," he said. "Come on! I'll drive the train, with you to help me. How pleased all the passengers will be!"

Hop, Skip, and Jump ran to the engine, and jumped into the cabin. There were four wheels there, like the steering wheels of motor-cars, and Hop had a good look at them.

Over one was written "Turn to the left," and

over another "Turn to the right." The third wheel had "Go fast" written over it, and the last wheel had "Start engine."

"Oh well, this all looks easy enough," said Hop, twisting the "Start engine" wheel. "Now we'll go on our travels once more!"

The train started off, rattle-clank, rattle!

All the passengers woke up and looked most surprised. They hadn't expected the train to go so soon. One of them looked to see why the driver had come back so quickly.

"Good gracious!" he cried, "those brownies are driving! We shall have an accident!"

Everyone looked over the edge of their carriages in alarm. Yes, sure enough, the brownies were driving the engine. Dear, dear, dear!

"We're coming to a curve!" said Skip, who was thoroughly enjoying himself. "Twist the 'Turn to the left' wheel, Jump!"

Jump did so, and the train went smoothly round the bend. The brownies felt very pleased with themselves indeed. Fancy being able to drive an engine without any practice!

"We *must* be clever!" they thought.

"There's a station coming!" shouted Jump. "Slow down, Hop, and stop, in case anyone wants to get out here."

But dear me! There wasn't any wheel that said "Slow down" or "Stop"! Even when they twisted the "Start engine" wheel backwards, the train didn't slow down.

Whiz-z-z! The station rushed by and the train didn't stop.

Some of the passengers were very angry, for they wanted to get out, and they began shouting and yelling at Hop for all they were worth. They made him so nervous that instead of twisting the "Turn to the right" wheel, when he came to another bend in the line, he twisted the "Go fast" wheel.

Br-rr-rr-rr! The engine leaped forward and raced along the rails as if it were mad. All the carriages rocked and rattled, and the passengers' hats flew off in the air.

"Hop! Hop!" shouted Skip, in a fright, "we shall have an accident. Make it go slow!"

But there wasn't any wheel that said "Go slow," and Hop didn't know what in the world to do. He twisted every wheel in turn, but nothing happened at all, except that the train seemed to go faster. The wind whistled past the brownies' ears, and took their breath away.

Stations whizzed past. The passengers forgot their anger in fear and clutched at the sides of their rocking carriages. A rabbit had his whiskers blown right off, and was terribly upset.

Then the train went up a big hill. It went more slowly, and some of the passengers wondered whether they would risk jumping out. There was a station at the top of the hill, and Hop read the name.

"Fiddlestick Field!" he cried. "Oh dear, this is where we get out. Oh, can't we stop the train somehow?"

But he couldn't, and the station went past. The train reached the hill-top, and began going down the other side.

The three brownies sat down suddenly, as the engine started tearing downhill.

"It's like a switchback!" groaned Hop. "Oh dear! It's climbing up another hill now!"

"And here's another station," said Skip, leaning out. "Oh my! Switchback Station! I hope to goodness we're not going to go up and down like this much longer. It makes me feel quite ill."

The train tore downhill again, then up and then down once more. The carriages followed in a rattling row, while all the passengers shrieked and shouted. Stations raced by, but the train didn't seem to think of stopping anywhere.

"Horrid little engine!" said Hop. "I believe it's thoroughly enjoying itself!"

"Oh my!" suddenly shouted Skip. "The engine's gone off the rails! Oh my!"

"And there's a pond in front of us!" yelled Jump. "Oh!"

Ker-splash! Ker-plunk! Into the pond went the engine, carriages and passengers. Everybody was tumbled, splash! into the pond, and the noise frightened all the ducks away to the bank.

"Splutter-splutter!" went everyone, floundering about in the shallow, muddy water. No one was hurt, but everybody was very, very angry.

"Catch those brownies!" they yelled, and made a grab at Hop, Skip, and Jump. "Spank them, and take them to prison!"

The brownies scrambled out of the pond as quickly as ever they could. They began to feel frightened when they heard the angry voices of all the dozens of passengers. There were rabbits, moles, weasles, Gigglers, two Clever People, a pedlar with a sack, and some queer people who didn't much look as if they belonged to anywhere.

They all scrambled out of the pond after the brownies and chased them. Down the lane went the three, followed by all the passengers.

"Stop them! Stop them!" they cried.

The brownies raced on. Soon they came to a queer little village, built entirely of large mush-rooms and toadstools. They had doors in the stalks, and windows and chimneys in the top part.

Little people came to the doors and looked out when they heard all the noise. They stared in astonishment at the sight of the three running brownies, followed by all the other queer people.

At the end of the village ran a stream. It was too wide and too deep for the brownies to cross, and they didn't know *what* to do.

"Quick, quick! Think of something!" cried Skip.

Hop looked round despairingly. The passengers were almost on them. Then a clever thought came to him.

He ran to a toadstool, snapped it off, put it upside down on the stream, and jumped into it. Skip and Jump sprang in just in time, pushed off from the bank, and left the passengers staring at them in dismay.

"Ha, ha!" called Hop, feeling very relieved. "You didn't get us *that* time!"

"No, but someone else will get you! Look behind you!" yelled the rabbit whose whiskers had been blown off.

The brownies looked on to the other bank, and

who do you think stood there? Why, three wooden-looking soldiers, all waiting for the toadstool boat to land!

Bump! The toadstool reached the shore. The soldiers sprang forward, caught hold of each of the brownies, and marched them off.

"Now, quick march!" said the soldiers sternly. "You'll go to prison till to-morrow morning, and then be brought before the judge for frightening our ducks, and for using one of our houses for a boat."

The brownies wriggled and struggled, but it was no good. They were marched into a toadstool marked PRISON, and there they were locked in for the night.

"Oh dear, dear, dear!" wept Jump, "I'm wet and cold and hungry. Hop, you've got us into trouble *again*!"

"Be quiet!" said Hop, who was feeling very much ashamed of himself and of his doings in the train.

"Good night," said Skip sadly. "I'm going to sleep to see if I can't find something to eat in my dreams."

And in two minutes the bad brownies were fast asleep.

Their Adventure in Toadstool Town

In the morning the brownies were awakened by someone opening their door. It was one of the soldiers. He gave them each a cup of water and some dry bread.

"In ten minutes you will be taken before the judge," he said.

The brownies shivered and shook. Whatever would happen to them?

"If only we'd waited for the engine-driver to finish his tea!" sighed Jump. "We'd be at Fiddlestick Field now, and the Saucepan Man would tell us the way to Witchland."

They all ate their bread and drank their water. Just as they had finished in came three soldiers.

They marched the brownies out of the toadstool, took them across the stream by a bridge, and into Toadstool Town. Everybody was staring at them and saying they were the bad brownies.

In the middle of the town a round space was cleared. At one end sat the judge, in an enormous wig. Just in front of him sat a lot of other people in wigs, all writing very fast indeed. All round sat the people of Toadstool Town, and the passengers who had come on the train with Hop, Skip and Jump the day before.

The brownies trembled when they saw them. They all looked so very cross.

"Prisoners," said the judge in a very loud voice, "stand up straight and answer my questions. Did you, or did you not, frighten our ducks yesterday?"

"I don't know," said Hop. "I frightened myself more than I frightened the ducks, I think!"

"That is no answer," said the judge, though Hop thought it was really rather a good answer. "Did you, or did you not, frighten our ducks?" he said again, turning to Skip.

"I didn't see any ducks, so I don't know," said Skip, who really hadn't noticed any ducks at all.

"That is no answer," said the judge again, and turned to Jump. "Did you, or did you not, frighten our ducks?"

"The ducks frightened *me*!" said Jump, who had fallen almost on top of a squawking duck when the train went into the pond.

"That is no answer," said the judge, who seemed to think nothing was an answer at all. He turned to the people gathered around.

"Did they, or did they not, frighten our ducks?" he asked.

"They *did*!" shouted everybody.

"That *is* an answer," said the judge in a satisfied voice. "What punishment shall they have?"

"Spank them!" cried the people.

"Very good," said the judge, writing something with a big pen in a big book. "Six spanks for each of them."

The brownies said nothing. They thought sadly that they seemed to get out of one spank into another.

The judge stopped writing and looked at the brownies.

"Stand up straight and answer my questions," he said. "Did you, or did you not, use one of our toadstool houses for a boat?"

"Yes," they answered, all together, "but we didn't know it was a house."

"Don't answer back," said the judge.

"We're *not*," said Hop indignantly.

"Are they, or are they not, answering back?" the judge asked all the people around.

"They are!" shouted the people, who seemed to be thoroughly enjoying themselves.

"What punishment shall they have for using one of our houses as a boat, and for answering back?" asked the judge.

"Spank them!" cried the people.

"Very good," said the judge, writing something with a big pen in a big book. "Six more spanks for each of them. Take them away."

Just as the soldiers were going to march them off the rabbit whose whiskers had been blown off stood up and waved his paw at the judge to attract his attention.

"Sit down," said the judge.

"I have something else to say against the prisoners," said the rabbit.

"Then don't sit down," said the judge, beaming on the rabbit. "What have you to say?"

"Please your worship," said the rabbit, "those bad brownies have done something *much* more serious than frightening ducks or answering back."

"What?" cried everyone.

"They took one of the Green Railway trains, and drove it!" said the rabbit. "And they aren't drivers, and they couldn't drive!"

"And they drove it into the pond!" shouted all the passengers. "And we got wet through!"

"Dear, dear," said the judge, looking very pleased to think he could punish the brownies for something else. "This matter must be looked into."

He turned to Hop.

"Can you drive an engine?" he asked him.

"If I couldn't drive an engine, how could I drive it into the pond?" asked Hop. "If you drive into a pond it shows you can drive, doesn't it, even if you drive in the wrong direction?"

Skip and Jump thought it was very clever of Hop to say that. Everyone looked very puzzled. The judge scribbled in his book, and frowned. Then he turned to the rabbit.

"Do you say these brownies can't drive?" he asked.

"Yes, I do," answered the rabbit, pulling at his whiskers that weren't there.

"And yet you say they *drove* the engine into the pond. Now this is an interesting point of law," said the judge, looking very learned. "The question is—can you say a person drives when he can't drive—no, that's not right—can you say a person can't drive and say at the same time that he did drive, but into a pond?"

Everyone looked at everyone else, and seemed to think hard.

"Well, anyway," said the rabbit crossly, "I say they aren't engine-drivers, and they shouldn't have driven our train yesterday."

"How do you know we aren't engine-drivers?" suddenly demanded Hop.

"Yes, how do you know?" asked Skip and Jump.

"Ah, yes, how do you know?" asked the judge, looking over his spectacles at the rabbit.

"Well, they aren't," said the rabbit sulkily. "Anyone who drives like they do isn't an engine-driver."

"Prove it!" cried Hop, suddenly getting an idea. "Let us show everyone here, the judge and all, whether we can drive or not."

Everyone got very excited, and began talking loudly.

"Silence," said the judge. "I have decided what to do. We will stop the next engine that comes to Toadstool Station. If these brownies show us they can drive it, we will give them only a light punishment. If they can't, we will put them in prison. When is the next train due?"

"At three o'clock in the afternoon," called someone.

"Very well," said the judge. "We will all be there. Take the prisoners away, guards, and give them twelve spanks each as a punishment for their other misdeeds."

The soldiers marched the brownies back to Toadstool Prison, gave them twelve spanks each, and left them.

"I really do believe we shall be able to get away to Fiddlestick Field this afternoon," said Hop, sitting down very carefully. "If that silly judge will only let us get in that engine, we'll be off like a shot."

"Yes, but look here," said Skip nervously, "you can't really drive, you know, and I'm getting tired of these adventures that land us into places we keep having to get away from. If you can't stop the engine again, goodness knows where we'll end at!"

"Well, do you want to stop in Toadstool Prison all your life?" asked Hop.

"No," sighed Skip. "I want to go back to Brownie Town, that's what *I* want!"

"Well, we can't do *that*," answered Jump, "so we've just got to put up with adventures like this."

All the morning the brownies sat in the Toadstool Prison, and waited for the afternoon. They peeped out through the little barred window now and then, and saw the people of Toadstool Town going about their work, doing their shopping, and gossiping with one another about the three bad brownies.

For dinner they were given a cup of water each and a big crust of bread. They ate the bread hungrily and drank the water, and then peeped out

of the window again to see if anything was happening.

People were beginning to gather round to see the brownies brought out to the railway station. They were talking and nudging each other.

"I don't like the people of this town very much," said Hop. "They stare so, and whisper to each other; I think someone ought to teach them manners."

"Ding-dong," struck a near-by clock.

"Two o'clock," said Skip. "Not much longer to wait, thank goodness! I'm longing to get out of this toadstool!"

At half-past two the soldiers came and took the brownies outside. They marched them through the town, with crowds of people following, all talking excitedly.

"*I* don't believe they can drive," said one.

"Nor do I," said another.

"They won't know how to start the engine!" cried a third.

"Then they'll soon be in prison again!" laughed a fourth.

Hop, Skip, and Jump began to feel rather nervous. Supposing they *couldn't* start the engine? How awful it would be! Oh dear, oh dear, how they wished they had never had to leave Brownie Town.

"Here's the station," said one of the soldiers, leading the brownies up some steps on to a little wooden platform.

All the people ran along beside the lines, and looked to see if the train was coming.

"I can see some smoke in the distance!" cried someone. "It will soon be here."

Puff-puff-puff-puff! Soon the little train came steaming up and stopped at Toadstool Town Station. The passengers got out, and stared in astonishment at the crowds all round.

The soldiers went up to the engine.

"Hi, you!" they called to the driver. "Get down a minute, please."

The surprised driver hopped out, and the soldiers explained to him about Hop, Skip, and Jump.

"But look here," said the driver, "suppose they go and smash up my engine?"

The soldiers looked taken aback! No one had thought of that.

"Here comes the judge," they said. "You ask him."

The driver bowed to the judge, and repeated his question.

"You should have thought of that before," answered the judge crossly. "We've got to go on with this now."

"Why, I only heard of this plan of yours just this minute," cried the driver indignantly. "How *could* I have thought of it before?"

"Don't answer back," snapped the judge, and turned to the brownies. "Now then," he said, "the time has come to show us whether you can drive or not. Get into the engine-cab."

The brownies jumped in.

"Drive to that bend," ordered the judge, "then reverse the engine and come back. Do you understand?"

"Yes, thank you," answered Hop, taking a good look at the wheels in the engine. "Hurrah!" he thought, "there's a 'STOP ENGINE' wheel this time. *I'll* be all right, I think!"

He twisted the "START ENGINE" wheel, and puff-puff-puff, off went the little engine by itself, for it had been uncoupled from the carriages.

"Not so fast!" shouted the judge.

Hop laughed, and twisted the "GO FAST" wheel. Off shot the engine faster than ever, past the rows of astonished people who were watching all along the lines.

"STOP! STOP! GO BACK!" shouted the crowds at the bend of the line, where Hop was supposed to go back.

"GOOD-BYE, GOOD-BYE," shouted the brownies, waving their hands in delight. "THANKS SO MUCH FOR LETTING US HAVE THIS ENGINE!"

They passed the last person by the line, and went tearing round the bend. They heard shouts and yells behind them, but they didn't even bother to look round.

"Hurrah! Hurrah!" shouted Skip. "We've got away! Good old Hop!"

Hop grinned. He was being very careful, for he didn't want to run any risks of being taken back to Toadstool Town. The engine went racing on, and passed one station after another. Jump read them out loud as they passed.

"We ought to be getting near Fiddlestick Field," said Skip at last. "Keep a good look out, Jump. Hadn't you better go a bit slower, Hop, so that we don't go rushing past the station!"

Hop twisted a wheel marked "GO SLOW," and the engine slowed down.

Two more stations were passed, and then Jump gave a squeak of delight, as the engine went up a steep hill.

"Fiddlestick Field!" he shouted. "Pull up, Hop, quick! we're really here!"

Hop stopped the engine, and the three brownies jumped out. No one was about at all. Evidently no train was expected at that time.

"Good for us!" grinned Hop. "We shan't have any questions asked!"

"I wonder what the people of Toadstool Town are thinking!" chuckled Skip. "They'll know we can drive all right *now!*"

"Come on," said Jump, running out of the station. "Let's find someone to ask where the Saucepan Man lives."

They went down a little winding lane, with honey-suckle hedges on each side. They hadn't gone far when they heard a most curious noise.

It was a clanging and a clanking, a jingling and a jangling.

"What in the world is that?" wondered Hop. "It sounds as if it's coming towards us. Perhaps we shall find out what it is, round the next corner."

Sure enough they did. They saw the most comical sight—it looked just like a walking mass of jingle-jangling saucepans!

"Goodness gracious!" said Hop in great astonishment. "What is it?"

"It's a whole heap of saucepans," said Skip, "and there's feet at the bottom. I can see them walking!"

When they got nearer they saw a tiny, bearded face peeping out of the crowd of saucepans, and discovered that it was a little man, hung from head to foot with saucepans of all sizes, shapes, and colours.

"It must be the Saucepan Man himself," said Hop, in delight. "What a bit of luck!"

Their Adventure with the Saucepan Man

THE three brownies ran up to the jingling-jangling little man.

"Hallo!" cried Hop. "Are you the Saucepan Man?"

The little man looked at him inquiringly.

"Hey?" he said. "What did you say?"

"Are you the Saucepan Man?" bawled Hop, over the jingling of scores of saucepans.

"No, I ain't got a sausage-pan!" answered the Saucepan Man, shaking his head so that the saucepans rattled tremendously.

"Sausage-pan! I never said a *word* about a sausage-pan," said Hop in surprise. "I said, 'Are you the Saucepan Man?'"

"I tell you I ain't got a sausage-pan," said the little man crossly, "I only sell saucepans, I do."

"He's deaf," said Skip, "and I don't wonder, with all those saucepans jangling round him all day."

Hop tried again. "Are you the Saucepan Man?" he bawled. "Can you hear me when I shout?"

"Yes, I think there's rain about," said the Saucepan Man, looking up at the sky wisely. "Come before evening too, likely enough."

"*You* try, Skip," said Hop, quite out of breath.

"WHERE ARE YOU GOING?" shouted Skip.

"Now don't be silly," answered the Saucepan Man sharply. " 'Tain't snowing, and you can see it ain't. Don't tell me any fairy-tales like that."

"CAN WE GO HOME WITH YOU?" asked Jump in his most enormous voice.

"No, my boots ain't new, but what's that to do with you, I'd like to know?" said the little man, looking crosser and crosser.

"Oh buttons and buttercups!" sighed Hop. "We'll never make him hear, while he's got all those saucepans jangling round him. Let's follow him and see if he's going home. Then if he takes off his saucepans, we'll try again then."

So the three brownies trotted behind the Saucepan Man, back down the lane again, and round by the station. There they saw the station-master and the porter, staring in great astonishment at the empty engine standing all by itself in the station.

"Gracious!" said Hop, "let's hope we don't get asked any awkward questions!"

The station-master saw them coming, and immediately rushed over to them.

"Pretend we don't understand," said Hop quickly to the others. "If we talk a lot of rubbish, he'll soon let us go."

"Hi! Hi!" called the station-master. "Do you know anything about this engine?"

Nobody answered anything.

"Are you dumb?" asked the station-master angrily. "Come now! Do you know anything about this engine, I say?"

"Kalamma Koo, chickeree chee," answered Hop solemnly.

"Krik-krik," said Skip.

"Caw," said Jump.

"*They* don't know anything, that's certain," said the station-master to the porter. "They're foreigners."

"Tanee jug jug jug?" said Hop, in an inquiring voice.

"It's all right," said the station-master. "I don't understand you. I'll have a word with this sauce-pan chap."

"Caw, caw," said Jump, and nearly made the others giggle.

The station-master poked the Saucepan Man in the ribs.

"Hi!" he cried, "do you know anything about this engine?"

"My name ain't Benjamin, and kindly take your fingers out of my waistcoat," said the Saucepan Man huffily.

The station-master groaned.

"Come on," he said to the porter. "They're quite mad—too mad to know anything about an engine, *any*way!"

They went off to the station again, and the three brownies breathed freely once more.

"That was a near squeak!" said Hop. "Come on, and let's follow the Saucepan Man."

On they went again, until at last the Saucepan Man came to a little tumbledown cottage, called Saucepan Cottage. It had old saucepans for its chimneys, and looked the funniest little place the brownies had ever seen. They followed the Saucepan Man inside. He looked at them in surprise.

"What do you want?" he asked.

Hop suddenly saw that the table was very dusty. He quickly wrote on it with his finger.

"We are three brownies who want to know the way to Witchland," he wrote. "The Very Wise Man told us to ask the Saucepan Man the way. Are you the Saucepan Man?"

" Course I am," said the little man; "can't you *see* that? Anyway, I don't know why you didn't ask me that in the road, instead of talking about sausage-pans and the weather."

He took off his saucepans and clattered them into a corner.

"I can tell you the way to Witchland all right," he said. "In fact, I'm on my way there to-morrow. You'd better come with me, you'll be safe then. Witches don't touch me, they don't."

"Why not?" asked Hop.

"Feel hot, do you?" said the little man. "Well, open the window then."

Hop sighed. It really was *very* difficult to talk to the Saucepan Man. He tried again.

"May we spend the night here?" he asked in his loudest voice.

"What's the matter with my right ear?" said the Saucepan Man, going to the looking-glass, and peering into it. "Nothing at all. Don't you be saucy, young man."

"I can't stand this!" groaned Hop to the others. "Haven't you got a note-book that we can write in?"

"Yes, *I* have!" cried Skip, pulling out an old note-book and a stumpy pencil. "Here you are; write in this, Hop."

Hop quickly wrote down his questions, and showed them to the Saucepan Man.

"Yes, you can stay here for the night," said the little man, "and I'll take you with me to-morrow. Find the cocoa-tin now, and make some cocoa, while I boil some eggs and make some toast."

The brownies hunted about for the cocoa, filled one of the many saucepans with milk and put it on the fire to boil.

Soon the four were enjoying boiled eggs, toast and cocoa, and the brownies began to think the Saucepan Man was a very jolly little man, for although he couldn't hear very well, he could tell lots of funny tales.

"Now to bed, to bed!" he said at last. "We've a long way to go to-morrow, and we must be up betimes."

He showed them a bedroom with a big bed in it, said good night, and shut the door.

"Well, I really feel we're on the way to find the Princess Peronel now," said Hop, as he got into bed.

"Yes, if the Saucepan Man takes us to Witchland, we've only got to find out where Witch Green-eyes lives, and then make up a plan to rescue her," said Skip sleepily.

"Well, good night," said Jump, yawning. All the brownies lay down, and fell fast asleep.

In the morning the Saucepan Man woke them, and they started off on their journey. They walked for miles across the country, calling at little cottages on the way, and selling saucepans.

Soon Hop had a good idea. He took out his little note-book and wrote in it.

"Let us carry your saucepans for you for a little while," Hop wrote. "You must be very tired, for the sun is hot."

The Saucepan Man gladly took off all his saucepans, and gave them to the three brownies. They divided them between them, and off they all went again, clinking and clanking for all the world as if they were saucepan men themselves.

Suddenly, as they were going along, a great shadow came over them, and made everything dark.

The brownies looked up and saw an enormous

yellow bird hovering over them. The Saucepan Man gave a frightened yell.

"Run!" he said, "run! It's the Dragon-bird that belongs to the Golden Dwarf. Don't let him get you!"

The brownies sped away to some trees. The Saucepan Man didn't seem to know *where* to go. He ran forwards and backwards, and sideways, and all the time the Dragon-bird hovered overhead like a great hawk.

Then zee-ee-ee! It swooped downwards so fast that its feathers made a singing noise. The brownies saw it get hold of the poor little Saucepan Man, and then the Dragon-bird rose into the air, taking him in its talons.

"Oh my! oh my!" cried Hop in despair. "It's got him! it's got him!"

"Poor little Saucepan Man," sobbed Skip, tears pouring down his face.

"Look! look! It's flying towards that hill over yonder," said Jump.

The brownies watched. On the top of the far-away hill was a castle. The Dragon-bird flew to the highest window there, landed, and disappeared into the castle.

"*Now* what are we to do?" said Hop mournfully.

"We can't go on and leave him," said Skip, drying his eyes. "Besides, we've got his saucepans."

"Oh, isn't it bad luck that this should happen, just as we were really on our way to Witchland!" sighed Jump. "Look at that signpost there. It says 'THIS WAY TO WITCHLAND' on it."

"Well, we'd better go to that hill over there," said Skip bravely. "We might be able to rescue the Saucepan Man *some*how. We simply *can't* leave him to that Dragon-bird and the Golden Dwarf."

"Come on then," said Hop, and off they all went, keeping a very sharp look-out in case the Dragon-bird came back again.

The hill was very much farther away than it looked. All the afternoon the brownies travelled, their saucepans clanking and jingling at every step.

"No wonder the Saucepan Man is so deaf!" said Hop. "It's all I can do to hear myself speak with all this noise going on."

Presently they came to a little cottage.

"Let's knock at the door," said Skip, "and see if we can get some food in exchange for a saucepan. I'm hungry."

They knocked. A dwarf opened the door and peered at them.

"What do you want?" he said.

"Do you want any saucepans?" asked Hop. "We've got some fine ones here."

"How much?" asked the dwarf.

"We'll give you a big one, if you'll give us a loaf, and some milk," said Hop.

The dwarf fetched them three cups of milk and a loaf of bread.

"Here you are," he said. "Now give me your biggest saucepan."

Hop gave him a fine blue saucepan.

"Who lives in that castle over there on that hill?" he asked.

"The Golden Dwarf," answered their customer. "Don't you go there, or you'll be captured by the Dragon-bird."

"Why does the Golden Dwarf capture people?" asked Skip.

"To eat," answered the dwarf. "Didn't you know *that*? Ah, he's a terrible fellow, the Golden Dwarf is, I can tell you. There's only one word that will stop him in his evil ways, but as he lives away up there in his high castle, that nobody can enter, he's safe!"

"What's the word?" asked Hop interestedly.

"Ho ho! don't you wish you could use it on the Golden Dwarf!" laughed the dwarf. "Well, I'll tell you. It's 'Kerolamisticootalimarcawnokeeto'!"

"Buttons and buttercups!" said Hop. "I'll never be able to say that!"

"We'll split it into three and each of us can remember a bit of it!" said skip cleverly.

The dwarf laughed, and said the long word again. Hop said the first piece over and over to himself, while Skip said the middle bit, and Jump repeated the last bit.

"Much good it'll do you!" said the dwarf. "Why, no one's ever even *seen* the Golden Dwarf since I've lived here—and I've been here a hundred and forty-three years come next November!"

The brownies sighed. Things seemed very difficult. They said good-bye, and left the cottage behind them.

"*Is* it any good going to the castle?" said Jump, who was beginning to feel very down in the dumps. "Suppose we all get caught and eaten."

"Cheer up," said Hop. "You can only get eaten *once*, you know!"

"Don't be silly," said Jump crossly. "I don't want to be eaten even once."

"Sh!" said Skip. "We're getting near the castle. Better keep a good look out."

"Bother the clanking saucepans," said Hop. "Shall we take them off and leave them here?"

"No," said Skip; "if that horrid Dragon-bird

appears again we'll pretend we're just a heap of old tins, and maybe it won't see us then."

Just as he spoke a shadow fell over them again. At once the three sank down to the ground beneath their saucepans, and lay quite still. The shadow grew blacker, and at last the Dragon-bird landed by them with a flop. It pecked at Skip's saucepans, and dented them badly. Then it spread its wings, rose into the air, and flew away again.

"Oh my stars!" said Jump, shaking like a jelly. "This is the sort of adventure that doesn't agree with me at all. Has that horrid bird gone?"

"Yes," said Hop. "It's a nasty-looking thing too, I can tell you. It's got scales as well as feathers, and a long tail. It must have thought we were piles of saucepans!"

"Come on while we're safe," said Skip.

They ran towards the castle, and, panting and breathless, flung themselves down at the foot of it.

"Isn't it a funny colour?" said Hop, looking at it closely. "It looks just like toffee!"

Skip broke a piece off and licked it.

"It *is* toffee!" he said. "My gracious! Fancy a castle built of toffee!"

"Toffee!" cried Jump in delight. "I say, how lovely! I'm going to have a jolly big bit!"

He broke off a fine fat piece and began chewing it. It was delicious.

"I suppose it was built by magic," said Hop. "I can't imagine *people* building it, can you? They'd get so terribly sticky."

"Well, don't let's forget about the Saucepan Man," said Skip, looking round about him. "I expect he's feeling very lonely and afraid."

"Let's explore round the outside of the castle," said Hop. "Maybe we can find some way of getting in, then."

Off went the brownies, after having carefully taken off the saucepans and hidden them under a bush. They were afraid that the Golden Dwarf might hear the clanking if they carried them about.

They marched off round the toffee castle, looking everywhere for a window or a door.

Not one was to be seen.

"Goodness!" said Hop at last. "No wonder nobody ever sees the Golden Dwarf, if there's no window and no door on the ground-floor."

"I don't believe there's any way of getting into the castle at all except by that window right at the very top," said Skip, craning his neck to see.

He was right. Not a door was to be seen, and no windows either, except the big one set right at the very top of the castle, where the

Dragon-bird had flown in with the Saucepan Man.

The brownies came back to their saucepans and sat down under the bush.

"Well, that *is* a puzzle," said Hop. "We haven't a ladder, and there's no door—so how ever *can* we get in?"

"We can't," said Jump. "The only thing left to do is to go back to that signpost, and take the road to Witchland."

"What, and leave the poor old Saucepan Man to be eaten by the Golden Dwarf?" cried Skip, who was very tender-hearted. "After he's been so very kind to us too!"

The others looked uncomfortable. They didn't like leaving their friend behind, but they didn't really see what else there was to do.

"Listen!" said Skip. "If you want something badly enough, you're *sure* to find out a way. Now let's just keep quiet and think very, *very* hard."

The three brownies put their heads on their hands, shut their eyes, and thought.

They thought and thought and thought.

The sun went down. Still the brownies thought.

The moon came up. Still the brownies thought.

Then Hop raised his head. "If only we could get something to climb up the wall with," he said. "But we haven't anything at all."

"Except silly old saucepans," said Jump mournfully.

"Yes—saucepans," repeated Hop. Then his eyes widened as a great thought came into his head.

"*Saucepans!*" he said again, and chuckled. Then he got up and did a little dance of joy. Skip and Jump stared at him in astonishment.

"Are you mad, Hop?" asked Skip.

"Or do you feel ill?" asked Jump.

"No, I'm not mad!" answered Hop. "I've only got that dancey feeling you get when you suddenly think of a perfectly splendid idea."

"What is it?" asked Skip and Jump together.

"Well, here we've been groaning and moaning because we've nothing to get us up the castle wall," said Hop, "and we've the very best thing in the world to get us up there—the saucepans!"

"Whatever *do* you mean?" asked Skip.

"*This* is what I mean," said Hop, and he picked up a saucepan. He held it upside down and drove the handle into the toffee wall. It went in quite easily, and stayed there, for the toffee held it tight.

"One step up," said Hop, and picked up another saucepan. He pushed the handle of that one in, a little way above the first one.

"Two steps up!" he cried. "*Now* do you see the idea?"

"Oh *yes!*" cried the other two. "What a good plan, Hop! We can climb up on the saucepans, if only the handles will hold all right!"

"The toffee will hold them," laughed Hop, who was beginning to feel very excited.

One by one the saucepans' handles were driven into the wall, so that every saucepan made a step higher than the last. They were quite firm and steady, and as the brownies were little and light, there was no fear of the steps breaking.

Higher and higher they went, until they had almost reached the window at the top. Jump carried the saucepans that were left, and passed them one by one to Skip, who passed them to Hop, who drove the handles into the wall.

"What a mercy we had so many saucepans!" whispered Skip.

"Yes, wasn't it?" said Hop. "I say! we're nearly at the top. Suppose the Golden Dwarf leans out of the window and sees us!"

"We'll say the magic word!" said Skip. "I know my bit all right."

"And I know mine!" said Jump.

"Well, we'll have to join the bits on very quickly when we say it," said Hop, "or else it won't sound like a word. Perhaps we'd better practise it before we go any further."

"Hurry up, then," said Skip; "I'm not very anxious to hang on to these saucepans all night."

Hop said his part of the magic word, Skip said the middle, and Jump joined in quickly with the end. After seven or eight times they managed to do it perfectly, and Hop thought they might go on.

They had just enough saucepans to reach to the window-ledge. At last Hop could peep over it and look into the room.

He saw a large room hung with golden curtains and spread with a golden carpet. In the middle of it, sitting on a stool, was the Saucepan Man, looking the picture of misery. He was all alone.

"Good!" said Hop, and whispered what he saw to the others. Then he peeped over the ledge again.

The Saucepan Man looked up, and when he saw Hop, he fell off his stool in astonishment.

"I must be dreaming," he said, and pinched himself very hard.

"Ow!" he said. "No, I'm not."

He ran to the window.

"Help me over," said Hop. "We've come to rescue you."

The Saucepan Man hauled him into the room, and then they helped Skip and Jump.

Quickly Hop wrote in his notebook to tell the Saucepan Man how they had come to him.

"You'd better escape at once, with us," wrote Hop. "For there's no knowing when that awful Dragon-bird will appear again, or the Golden Dwarf."

"Ugh! don't talk of them," begged the Saucepan Man. "I shall never forget being carried off in those talons. When I got here the Golden Dwarf came and looked at me, and said I wouldn't be plump enough to eat for a week."

The brownies shivered.

"Come on," said Hop, running to the window. "Let's escape whilst we can."

He had just got one leg over the window-sill, when heavy foot-falls outside the door made his hair stand on end.

"Oh!" whispered the Saucepan Man. "Hide quick! It's the Golden Dwarf."

The brownies dived behind one of the curtains just as the door opened. In came a queer creature, not much bigger than the brownies, who looked as if he were made of solid gold. Hop thought he looked more like a statue than a live person.

"I smell brownies!" said the Golden Dwarf suddenly, and sniffed the air.

The three brownies trembled.

"Remember the magic word," whispered Hop anxiously. "It's our only chance."

"I SMELL BROWNIES!" said the Golden Dwarf again, and strode over to the shaking curtain.

He pulled it aside. Out sprang Hop, Skip, and Jump. "Kerolamisti——" shouted Hop.

"Cootalimar——" went on Skip.

"Cawnokeeto!" finished Jump.

The Golden Dwarf stared at them in terror.

"The Word! The Word!" he cried, and pulled at his hair. Then he uttered a deep groan, jumped into the air, and vanished completely.

The brownies and the Saucepan Man stared at the place where the Golden Dwarf had stood. Nothing happened. He didn't come back.

"You've done the trick!" said the Saucepan Man. "He's gone for good!"

"Hurrah!" cried Hop. "Thank goodness we remembered the magic word! Come on, Saucepan Man—let's get away from this horrid castle!"

Over the window-sill they clambered, and were soon scrambling down the saucepans as fast as they could go. "We'll leave them there," said the Saucepan Man. "I don't want to waste any more time here, in case the Dragon-bird comes back."

So off they all went in the moonlight to the sign-post pointing to Witchland.

Their Adventure with the Labeller and the Bottler

THEY hadn't gone very far when the Saucepan Man began to yawn.

"I'm *so* sleepy," he said, "and it really must be very late. What about getting underneath a bush, and going to sleep till morning?"

The brownies thought it would be a very good idea. So they all cuddled together beneath a bush, and went fast asleep till the sun rose.

"Wake up! wake up!" cried Hop. "It's time to go on our way to Witchland and rescue the Princess Peronel."

The others woke with a jump. They washed in a near-by stream, picked some blackberries for breakfast, and went on towards the sign-post.

Suddenly there came over them a great black shadow.

"Oh! oh!" yelled the Saucepan Man in terror, "it's the Dragon-bird again. Run! Run!"

The brownies ran helter-skelter to some bushes. The black shadow grew darker.

Zee-ee-ee! The Dragon-bird landed on the ground by them with a thud.

"Where is my master? Where is my master?" it cried in a croaking voice.

"We have said a magic word and made him vanish for ever!" shouted Hop bravely. "And if you don't leave us alone, we'll make *you* vanish too, you horrid Dragon-bird."

"No, no!" shrieked the bird. "Oh, most powerful wizard, let me serve *you*, now that my master, the Golden Dwarf, is gone. Let me be your slave."

"Gracious!" said Hop. "Here is a to-do! Goodness knows we don't want a Dragon-bird always at our heels, begging to be our slave."

The Saucepan Man, who seemed to hear the Dragon-bird quite well, crawled out from under his bush and walked up to it.

"Go away!" he said. "If we want you we will call you. Don't come bothering us now, or we will make you disappear, as we did your master."

"I will come if ever you want me," croaked the bird sadly. "I will await that time."

It spread its wings, rose into the air, and in a few moments was out of sight.

"That was rather a nasty shock," said Hop. "I quite thought it would take us all away again. Ugh! I hope we never see the ugly thing any more!"

"So do *we*!" said Skip and Jump.

"Come on," said the Saucepan Man, and once more the four set off to the sign-post.

At last they reached it, and set off down the road towards Witchland.

"Don't you bother to come with us," said Hop to the Saucepan Man. "We can find our way quite well, now."

"No, I can't hear any bell," said the Saucepan Man, standing still to listen. "You must be mistaken."

"Oh dear, you *are* deaf!" sighed Hop, and quickly wrote down what he had said.

"Ho, ho!" laughed the Saucepan Man. "So you think you could find the way by yourself, do you? Ho! ho! You just follow me, and you'll soon see you couldn't find the way alone!"

No sooner had he said that than the four travellers came to a river. Over it stretched a graceful bridge; but, to the brownies' surprise, no sooner did they get near it than the end nearest to them raised itself and stayed there.

"How annoying of it!" said Hop in surprise. "What does it do that for? We can't get across!"

"Don't worry!" said the Saucepan Man. He looked about in the ground and picked up four tiny blue stones. He threw them into the river one after the other, saying a magic word at each of them.

At once the end of the bridge came down again, and rested on the bank.

"There you are," said the Saucepan Man. "Now we can cross."

The brownies ran across quickly, just in case the bridge took it into its head to do anything funny again.

They hadn't gone very far beyond the bridge before they came to a forest so dark and so thick that the brownies felt sure they couldn't possibly get through it. They tried this way and that way, but it was all no good; they could find no path.

The Saucepan Man watched them, laughing.

Then he quickly ran to a big white stone lying near by and lifted it up. Underneath it lay a coil of silver string. The Saucepan Man took it up and tied one end to a tree-trunk.

Then he said a magic rhyme, and immediately, to the brownies' tremendous surprise, the string uncoiled and went sliding away all by itself into the dark forest.

"Follow it quickly!" cried the Saucepan Man, and ran into the forest.

The silver string gleamed through the bushes and trees, and led the brownies by a hidden, narrow path through the dark forest. On and on they went, following the silver thread, until at last they reached the end of the trees, and stood in sunshine once more.

"I don't know what we should do without you," shouted Hop to the Saucepan Man. "We should never have known the way!"

"*Who's* making hay?" asked the Saucepan Man, staring all round about him.

"No one!" shouted Hop, and wrote in his note-book to tell the Saucepan Man what he was talking about.

Presently they set off again. In the distance they saw an enormous hill. As they drew nearer the brownies saw it gleaming and glittering, as if it were made of ice.

"Glass," explained the Saucepan Man, as they drew near.

"I wonder how we get up *that*!" said Hop.

The brownies tried to climb it, but as fast as they tried, down they came, ker-plunk, to the bottom!

"Tell us how to get up!" Hop wrote in his note-book, to the Saucepan Man.

Their guide smiled. He took six paces to the left, picked up a yellow stone, and aimed it carefully at a notch in the glass hill.

146

Directly it struck the notch, a door slid open in the hillside, and the brownies saw a passage leading through the glass hill.

"It's easier to go through than up," smiled the Saucepan Man, leading the way.

The passage was very queer, for it wound about like a river. The sides, top, and bottom were all glass, and reflected everything so perfectly that the brownies kept walking into the walls, and bumping their noses.

They were very glad when at last they came out at the other side of the hill. In front of them towered a great gate, and on it was written in iron lettering:

WITCHLAND

"At last!" said Hop. "Now we really have arrived!"

"Here I must leave you," said the Saucepan Man sadly. "I cannot go in, and I don't know how *you'll* get in either. But you are so clever, that maybe you'll find a way. Now I must go back and make some more saucepans to sell."

"Thank you for bringing us here," wrote Hop in his note-book. "We are sorry to say good-bye."

"So am I," said the Saucepan Man, with tears in his eyes. "Thank you very much for all your goodness to me in rescuing me from the Golden Dwarf."

"Don't mention it," said the brownies politely. Then the Saucepan Man shook hands solemnly with them all, and said good-bye.

"Good-bye, good-bye!" called the brownies, as he went towards the glass hill.

He turned round.

"What sort of pie?" he called in surprise.

"Oh buttons and buttercups, isn't he deaf!" said Hop, and waved to the Saucepan Man to go on.

They watched him disappear into the hill.

"Nice old Saucepan Man," said Skip. "Wish he was coming to Witchland with us."

"I wonder how we get in!" said Hop, looking at the tall gates.

148

"Don't know," said Skip. "We'd better wait until someone goes in or out, and then try and slip in as the gates open. Let's sit down under this may-tree and wait."

They sat down and waited.

Nobody went either in or out of the gates. The brownies felt very bored.

Hop looked all round to see if anyone was in sight. He suddenly saw something in the distance.

"Look!" he said. "There's a procession or something coming. We could easily slip in with that, when the gates open for it, couldn't we?"

"Yes!" said Jump. "Let's wait quietly and then try our luck."

The procession came nearer. At the same time there came somebody from the opposite direction. Skip looked to see who it was.

"It's a little brown mouse!" he said in surprise. "I wonder what a mouse is doing here! He seems to be carrying a heavy sack, look!"

The others looked. The little mouse was certainly carrying a sack that seemed far too heavy for him.

The procession and the mouse reached the place where the brownies sat, just at the same moment. The procession was made up of all sorts of queer people carrying precious rugs, caskets, and plants.

"Going in to sell them to the witches, I suppose!" whispered Hop. "Look! the gates are opening! Get ready to slip inside!"

But just at that moment the mouse gave a shrill squeak.

The brownies looked round. They saw that the sack had fallen off the little mouse's back, and that hundreds of green labels were flying about all over the place.

"Oh! oh! What shall I do?" squeaked the mouse. "I shall be late, I know I shall!"

The brownies jumped up.

"Let us help you to pick them up!" said Hop. "It won't take a minute."

"We must hurry, though," said Skip, "or we shan't get in whilst the gates are open."

The brownies quickly picked up the labels and filled the mouse's sack again. He was very grateful indeed.

"Don't mention it," said Hop, and turned to the gates of Witchland.

Clang! They shut, for the last of the queer procession had gone in!

"Oh my!" said Hop in dismay, "now we've lost our chance!"

The little mouse looked very upset. "Did you want to get in?" he asked.

"Yes," said Hop. "But it doesn't matter—we'll wait till someone else wants to go in again, and the gates open."

"I wish we could find something to eat," sighed Skip. "I'm getting so *dreadfully* hungry!"

"Won't you come home with me for a while?" asked the mouse. "I'm sure my master, the Labeller, would give you something to eat, as you've been so kind in helping me."

"Well, thank you very much," said Hop. "But what a funny name your master has—the Labeller! Whatever does he label?"

"Oh, whenever people are crosspatches, or spiteful, or horrid in any way," said the mouse, "they are taken to the Labeller, and he puts a label round their neck that they can't get off. Then everyone knows what sort of person they are, and if they're very nasty, people avoid them as much as they can."

"That seems a very good idea," said Skip, as the brownies followed the mouse down a pathway. "Do they have to wear the labels all their lives?"

"That depends," said the mouse, trotting down a hole in a bank. "You see, directly they stop being horrid, their label flies off, and goes back to the Labeller! If they go on being horrid for the rest of their lives, the label *never* flies off."

"I say! The Labeller won't label *us*, will he?" asked Hop anxiously, as they all trotted down the hole after the mouse.

"Oh no!" said the mouse. "*You're* not horrid at all—you're very nice."

The passage was lighted with orange lights, and beneath every light was a little door. Each door had a name-plate on, and the brownies read them all as they passed by.

"Here's a funny one!" said Hop. "The Bottler. I wonder what he bottles!"

"Oh, and here's the Labeller!" said Skip. "The mouse is going inside."

They followed him and found themselves in a cosy little room where a bright fire was burning. By a little table sat a fat old man with spectacles on. He was printing names on labels in very small and beautiful letters.

"Come in, all of you," he said in a kind voice. "I don't know who you are, but you're very welcome."

The brownies said good day politely and told him who they were.

"Where do you come from?" he asked.

"Brownie Town," they answered.

"Well, what are you doing *here*, then?" asked the Labeller in surprise.

The brownies went very red. Nobody spoke for a minute, and then Hop told the Labeller all about the naughty trick they had played at the King's party, and how the little Princess had been spirited away.

"Dear, dear, dear," said the Labeller, "that was a very silly thing to do. Perhaps I'd better label you all silly, had I?"

"No, thank you," said the brownies quickly. "We aren't silly any more. We're sorry for what we did, and we're trying to find the Princess and rescue her." The Labeller got out some buns and told the little mouse to make some milk hot.

"Sit down," he said, "and have something to eat. I'm sure it was very kind of you to help my little servant to pick up all the labels he had dropped."

The brownies each took a bun and said "Thank you."

"And when are you going back to Brownie Town?" asked the Labeller. "When you've rescued the Princess?"

"No," answered Hop sadly, "we can't. The King said we weren't to go back until we had found our goodness—and people can't find their goodnesses, of course—so we're afraid we'll *never* be able to go back."

"But of *course* you can find your goodness if you've got any!" said the Labeller. "Why, my brother, the Bottler, can easily give you it if you've any that belongs to you. He bottles up all the goodness in the world, you know, and then, when anyone starts being peevish and grumpy, he seeks out his messenger—my mouse's cousin—to drop a little out of one of the bottles of goodness into something the peevish person is drinking. Then the grumpy person begins to smile again, and thinks the world is a jolly old place, after all."

"Dear me!" said the brownies, in the greatest surprise. "Is that really so?"

"And do you mean to say that if we've done any good deeds, for instance, the Bottler has got them boiled down and bottled up in a jar?" asked Skip in excitement. "Bottles that we can take away?"

"Oh rather," said the Labeller, taking another bun. "With your own names on and everything."

"Well! If that isn't splendid!" cried Hop in delight. "*Could* we go and see if the Bottler's got any of our goodness bottled up?"

"Finish your milk and buns first," said the Labeller, "then you can go."

The brownies finished their food and jumped up.

"Well, good-bye," said the Labeller, shaking

hands with them. "The mouse will show you the right door. Good luck to you."

Off went the brownies in a great state of excitement. They almost trod on the mouse's tail, they were in such a hurry.

They came to the little door marked "The Bottler." They knocked.

"Come in," said a voice.

They went in, and saw a room like the Labeller's. It was full of thousands of bottles standing on hundreds of shelves.

The Bottler was very like the Labeller, except that he was a good deal fatter.

"What can I do for you?" he asked.

"Please," said Hop in a shaky voice, "please have you any goodness of ours bottled up?"

"Who are you?" asked the Bottler kindly.

"Hop, Skip, and Jump, three brownies from Brownie Town!" answered Hop.

"Hm-m-m, let me see," said the Bottler, putting a second pair of spectacles on. He walked up to a shelf labelled "Brownies" and began peering at the bottles.

The brownies waited impatiently. Oh, if only, only, only a bottle of their goodness could be found, they could go back to Brownie Town.

"Ha! Here we are!" said the Bottler, at last

pouncing on a little yellow bottle. It had something written on the label that was stuck round it. The Bottler read it out:

" 'This goodness belongs to Hop, Skip, and Jump. It was made when they rescued a mermaid from the castle of the Red Goblin.' "

"Oh fancy!" said Jump. "I *am* glad we rescued Golden-hair!"

"Dear me, here's another bottle, too," said the Bottler. He picked up a little green bottle, and read out a label.

" 'This goodness belongs to Hop, Skip, and Jump. It was made when they helped a little girl to escape from the Land of Clever People.' "

"Buttons and buttercups!" said Hop. "That's *two* bottles to take back."

"And here's a third bottle!" suddenly said the Bottler, and picked up a red bottle.

" 'This goodness belongs to Hop, Skip, and Jump. It was made when they rescued the Saucepan Man from the Golden Dwarf!' " read the Bottler.

"How perfectly lovely!" cried Jump. "That's a bottle each! How glad I am that we *did* help those people when we had the chance."

"Here you are," said the Bottler, handing them the bottles. "Take care of them, for they'll take you safely back to Brownie Town. Now good-bye. I'm glad to have been of some use to you!"

"Good-bye, and thank you very much," called the brownies, and hurried out into the passage with their precious bottles. The little mouse was outside, waiting for them.

"If you like, I'll show you a secret way into Witchland," he said. "I'd be pleased to help you any way I could."

Hop hugged the kind little mouse.

"Please show us," he said. He put his bottle into his pocket, and followed the mouse up the passage.

The mouse ran down passage after passage, and at last went up a very steep one.

"This leads into a witch's house," he whispered. "There's a big mouse-hole that comes out into the cellar. You can squeeze through it."

"Thank you," said Hop. "Tell me, little mouse, what witch lives here?"

"Witch Green-eyes," whispered the mouse.

"Witch Green-eyes!" said the brownies in surprise. "Just the very witch we want!"

They said good-bye to the mouse, squeezed through the hole, and found themselves in a dark, smelly cellar.

"Well," said Hop, "now we'll soon see if we can't rescue Princess Peronel!"

Their Adventure in the House of Witch Green-eyes

EVERYWHERE was dark, and the brownies had to feel their way carefully in case they tumbled over anything. Suddenly they heard footsteps, and saw the light of a candle coming down some steps at one end of the cellar. "It's the witch herself!" whispered Hop in great excitement. "Keep still, whatever you do!"

Sure enough, it *was* Witch Green-eyes. The brownies could see her eyes gleaming green like a cat's, as she walked down the cellar.

"Now where did I put that barrel of gold?" she muttered. "Surely it was somewhere in this corner?"

She was coming nearer to the brownies. They shrank back into the shadows in fear.

"I *must* find that gold," they heard her mutter. "Now where is it? Ah! here it is!"

She stopped just by them and began jingling money in a barrel. The brownies kept as still as still.

The witch began counting out the money. "One—two—three—four—five."

The brownies made never a sound. They held

their breath and hoped the witch would soon go.

After she had counted out a hundred pieces of gold she picked up her candle, took the bag of money, and turned to go.

She shuffled her way across the cellar floor, muttering to herself. The brownies began to breathe freely again, for they felt they were safe.

But just at that moment something happened.

Skip put his hands over his mouth and nose, and held them tight.

"Whatever is the matter?" whispered Hop.

"I'm going to sneeze!" stuttered Skip.

Now the more you try to stop a sneeze the bigger it is when it *does* come. And when Skip's sneeze came it was ENORMOUS.

"A-TISHOO-SHOO!" he sneezed, and nearly jerked his head off.

The witch dropped her bag of money in amazement and held her candle up to see whatever was in the cellar.

"Quick—the mouse-hole!" whispered Hop, and the brownies ran to where they thought it was.

But oh dear me, they couldn't find it *any*where, not anywhere at all.

The witch came down the cellar again, holding her candle up high, and looking as fierce as ever a witch could look.

"Ho! ho!" she said as she saw the scurrying brownies. "And what are *you* doing here, I should like to know?"

"N-n-nothing m-much," answered Hop, wondering wherever the mouse-hole was. "J-just looking for spiders, you know."

"Looking for my *gold*, more likely," growled the witch. "You wouldn't be down in my cellar for *spiders*, you little squiggling brownies. You come along upstairs, and I'll show you a better place for spiders!"

She took hold of them and pushed them in front of her.

"Up the steps you go," she cried, her green eyes looking more like a cat's than ever.

The frightened brownies rushed up the steps and found themselves in a large kitchen.

"Now," said the witch with a nasty sort of smile, "you'll find plenty of cobwebs about my kitchen. Just go and look for spiders behind them, whilst I ask my black cat to tell me exactly what you *were* in the cellar for. It's not much good asking *you*, I can see, as you seem to think of nothing but spiders."

The poor little brownies had to go and poke about in the thick cobwebs that hung in the dark corner of the kitchen. They couldn't bear it, for the spiders were large, and very, very creepy-crawly.

The witch called her black cat.

"Cinder-boy, Cinder-boy!" she cried.

In walked an enormous cat with eyes as green as the witch's.

"Sit in the magic circle, Cinder-boy," said the witch, "and tell me the answers to my questions."

The cat went and sat down in the middle of a circle chalked on the kitchen floor. It closed its eyes and swished its tail about.

"Oh, Cinder-boy," cried the witch, waving her stick over him, "tell me, I pray you, what has brought these three brownies here?"

"They come to rescue the Princess Peronel," replied the cat in a deep, purring voice.

"Nasty old tell-tale," whispered Hop to Skip. "Look out for that spider! It's crawling up your leg."

"Ho! ho!" laughed the witch. "To rescue the Princess Peronel! That's a great joke indeed! Now tell me, Cinder-boy, does anyone in Fairyland know they have come here?"

"No one knows," answered Cinder-boy. "No one will ever know if you keep them here for ever."

"I don't like that cat," said Skip. "It knows a lot too much for a cat."

"Ha, ha, ho, ho!" laughed the witch again. "Thank you, Cinder-boy. Now I know what to do with these horrid little brownies. I'll put them in the High Tower with the Princess Peronel, and I won't let them go till they have made her do what I want."

She turned to the brownies.

"Come," she said. "I will take you to the Princess you want to rescue. I will chain you up with her, and then you shall see whether it is an easy matter or not to come to Witchland and rescue a Princess held by Witch Green-eyes."

She hustled them out of the room to where a spiral staircase ran up and up and up. The brownies climbed it, and thought surely it would never come to an end. But at last, after Hop had counted two thousand six hundred and eighty-four steps, he saw a low door in front of him, heavily bolted, locked and padlocked.

The witch unlocked and unbolted the door and pushed the brownies inside. There they saw a sight that made their hearts leap for joy—for the little Princess Peronel was in the room, sitting at a window looking longingly out.

She turned as they came in, and the brownies saw that golden chains were round her legs and bound her to a staple in the wall. It made them feel very angry and very sad at the same time.

"Here you are!" said the witch. "Here's the Princess you came to rescue! Now just you make her do what I want her to do, and I'll set you free! If not, I'll keep you here for the rest of your lives!"

She quickly slipped a chain round the legs of each brownie, so that they were bound to the wall like the Princess. Then she gave a wicked chuckle and went out of the door. They heard her locking and bolting it.

"Hallo," said the brownies to the surprised Princess.

"Have you *really* come to rescue me?" asked Peronel eagerly.

"We came to Witchland to try," said Hop; "but the old witch caught us too soon."

"Oh dear!" said the Princess sadly. "I wonder if I'll ever be rescued. I've been here such a long time. You *won't* try to make me do what the nasty old witch wants, will you?"

"What does she want you to do?" asked the brownies.

"She keeps telling me I must marry the old wizard who lives next door to her," sighed Peronel. "He'll give her a thousand bags of gold if I do marry him."

"Good gracious!" cried Hop, as angry as could be. "How *dare* she ask you to do such a thing! We must certainly rescue you."

"But how?" asked the little Princess. "I don't think *any*one could escape from this high tower!"

"Besides, we're chained up," said Hop mournfully.

Jump went to the window and looked out. They were certainly in a very, very high tower. The windows were barred too. The door was locked and bolted, and the prisoners were chained. It seemed hopeless. They would just have to stop there for always!

Hop went carefully round the room, with his chain clanking round his leg, and felt the walls and the door. They were all as solid as could be. The window, too, was far too high for anyone to hear them calling. All Witchland lay spread out below like a map.

The brownies sat down on the floor in despair.

"Tell me how you came here," said the Princess. "I've been so dull here all by myself, and I'd like to hear your adventures."

So the brownies began to tell them. They began at the beginning, and told of the Cottage without a Door, the Castle of the Red Goblin, the Land of the Giants, the Clever People and the Gigglers. Then they told her of Toadstool Town and their adventure on the Green Railway.

Peronel loved it all.

"Go on," she said. "Tell me more."

So they told her of the Saucepan Man, and how they had rescued him from the Dragon-bird and the Golden Dwarf.

"And," said Hop, "we got an awful fright as we were going along the day after we had rescued him, because the Dragon-bird came *again*!"

"Again!" cried the Princess in horror. "Did it carry any of you away?"

"No, it wanted its master," explained Hop, "and

165

when it couldn't find him, it said it would be our slave, and come whenever we wanted it, if only we'd call."

"*Well*," said the Princess, "why *don't* you call the old Dragon-bird? It might help us, mightn't it?"

"Buttons and buttercups!" squeaked Hop in excitement. "Oh buttons and buttercups! Fancy us not thinking of that! Oh Princess Peronel, what a good thing you thought of it! Of *course* we'll call the good old Dragon-bird! It might get us help, even if it couldn't help us itself."

The brownies were tremendously excited, and so was the Princess. Hop went to the window, and called out as loudly as he could:

"Dragon-bird! Dragon-bird! Come to your new masters! We need you!"

They waited. Nothing happened. No sound of rushing wings came. Everyone felt very disappointed. Then Skip looked out of the window again. He gave a cry of delight.

"I believe the Dragon-bird is coming!" he called. "Look! Far away, ever so high up in the air!"

Hop looked. He saw a tiny black speck far away.

"I'll call again!" he said. And once more he cried out to the Dragon-bird to come.

The speck grew larger and larger. Then zee-ee-ee! The Dragon-bird swooped down from the sky and landed with a thud on their window-sill.

"Masters, I come!" it croaked. "What can I do for you?"

"Listen, Dragon-bird," said Hop excitedly. "We are prisoners here. Can you find some way of saving us?"

"Let me come into the room with you," said the bird. "I can talk with you better then."

Cric-crac-cric-crac! It nipped each bar at the window with its strong beak, and broke them off one by one. Then, the window clear of bars, the Dragon-bird hopped through the opening and stood on the table.

"What a peculiar-looking bird!" said the Princess, not at all afraid of the enormous creature. She went up to it and patted it.

The Dragon-bird shivered all over with delight.

"Little lady," it croaked, "you are the first person who has ever patted me! I will do anything to rescue you and your friends!"

"Well, you can rescue us easily enough!" said the Princess, patting the bird again. "Do you think you could manage to carry us away on your back?"

"I don't know," said the Dragon-bird doubtfully. "There's four of you. I've never carried more than one before. I'm not an omnibus, you know."

"No, you're an aeroplane!" said Hop. "Come on, Dragon-bird! Let us tie ourselves on to your back and go. The old witch may be back at any moment!"

The Princess patted the bird again. It was so pleased that it gave a crow of delight.

"Good gracious!" said Hop in horror. "What an awful noise, Dragon-bird! You'll have the witch here in no time if you do that!"

"What about our chains?" asked Skip. "How can we get rid of those?"

The bird leant forward and took Peronel's chains in his beak.

Cric-crac! It bit them in two!

"My!" cried Jump. "What a help you are, to be sure!"

Then the Dragon-bird bit all the brownies' chains in two and they were once more free.

"Now go to the window-sill," said Hop, trying to push the bird off the table, "and we'll get on your back one by one."

The bird hopped over to the window.

"You needn't tie yourselves on my back," it

croaked, "I will make four strong feathers stand upright, and you can hold on to those."

Peronel stood on a chair, climbed up on to the bird's back, took hold of a fine strong feather, and settled herself comfortably. The others followed.

"Have we got everything?" asked Hop, looking behind. "Our bottles of goodness are in our pockets, aren't they?"

"Yes," said Skip joyously. "Oh, isn't it grand, Hop? We've got the Princess safe, and we've got the bottles of goodness too, so that soon we'll be in our own dear little cottage once more!"

"Hold tight," said the bird suddenly. Everyone held tightly to their feathers. Then off they went into the air, far above the spires and towers of Witchland carried strongly along on the big broad back of the Dragon-bird.

It was fine. The bird flapped its wings steadily, and the air rushed whistling by their ears. Witchland was left behind, and the Glass Hill. They were going very fast indeed, and didn't they enjoy it!

They had been flying along steadily for some time when Hop happened to look behind them. Witchland could hardly be seen—it was just a blur in the distance.

But out of that blur Hop suddenly saw a little

black spot come. He strained his eyes to see what it was.

"Look, Skip," he said, pointing behind. "Can you make out what that is? Is it another bird, or *what* is it?"

Skip looked, and so did Peronel and Jump, but none of them could make out what it was.

'We shall soon see," said Hop. "It's catching us up. I expect it is a bird of some sort."

"Then it won't catch us up!" croaked the Dragon-bird. "I fly faster than any bird living."

"Well, but it *is* catching us up," said Hop, as the black spot grew larger.

The Dragon-bird looked round to see this fast-flying bird. Then he gave such a jump and such a cry of alarm that his four passengers were very nearly jolted off. Hop just saved Skip by catching hold of one of his legs and pulling him safely up again.

"*Don't* do that," said Hop to the Dragon-bird very severely. "Or at any rate be polite enough to tell us when you're going to do it."

"I couldn't help it!" croaked the Dragon-bird. "Do you know what that black speck following us is?"

"No, what?" asked everybody.

"It's old Witch Green-eyes on her magic

170

carpet!" panted the bird. "She must have missed you and come after you!"

"Oh, quick, quick, quick!" cried the brownies in fright. "Fly your fastest, Dragon-bird. Quick, quick!"

The Dragon-bird flapped its wings even faster and tore through the air so swiftly that Peronel's hair shot out straight behind her.

Behind them came that horrid black speck, getting bigger and bigger every minute that passed.

"We can't be very far away from Fairyland," shouted Hop. "We must have gone miles and miles already. Go on, brave Dragon-bird."

On they went, and on and on. But every time they looked behind they shivered—for the black speck was so much larger.

At last they could see quite plainly that it was a witch sitting on a flat magic carpet that raced through the air in a most marvellous way.

"Oh buttons and buttercups!" groaned Hop in despair. "Fancy, to be so near Fairyland, and yet to be so near being captured, too! Go on, Dragon-bird; keep it up!"

"I—can't—go—on—much—longer!" panted the bird. ' I'm so—tired and—you're—allso-heavy!" He ran the last words together, for he was very nearly breathless. The brownies could feel his heart beating bump—bump—bump in his body and they felt terribly sorry for him.

Suddenly Hop gave a shout of joy.

"Look! look!" he cried, pointing before them. "There's the palaces of Fairyland. We're nearly there, we're nearly there! Go on, dear old Dragon-bird!"

The bird's wings were flapping more slowly, but he put on an extra spurt when he heard the good news.

Behind them, closer and closer, came the old Witch Green-eyes on her carpet. She was so excited that she stood up and her hair flew behind her in the wind like long black snakes.

"I'll catch you, I'll catch you!" she shouted. The brownies could just hear her voice, and they shivered.

Nearer and nearer she came. And nearer and nearer came Fairyland.

"I—can't—fly—any—more!" gasped the bird suddenly, and began to drop downwards.

"Go on, go on!" shouted Hop, "you can, you can! Look, there's the walls of Fairyland; you've only got to fly over them and you're safe!"

The bird made for the walls, tried to fly over them—and just missed them. It sank to the ground just outside Fairyland, and lay there exhausted, whilst its four passengers scrambled off its back in dismay.

The Princess covered her eyes as she saw the witch rapidly coming down to them on her magic carpet. She was brave enough not to cry, but she felt very like it indeed.

"We'll fight for you!" said Hop, putting his arm round her. "Don't be afraid!"

Bump! The witch landed just in front of them, jumped off her carpet, and ran over to them.

"Ho! ho!" she laughed, "so I've caught you after all!"

The brownies looked at her in despair.

"Keep away from the Princess," shouted Hop bravely, "or we'll fight you."

"Pooh! You haven't anything to fight with!" said the witch, grabbing at the Princess.

"Oh, *haven't* we!" cried Hop, and took out his bottle of goodness. "We'll whack you with these bottles of goodness, if you dare to touch the Princess!"

The witch turned from the frightened Princess, and stared at Hop in amazement.

"Bottles of goodness!" she cried. "Where did you get *those* from?"

"The Bottler, of course!" said Hop, swinging his bottle round as if to hit the witch.

"Don't do that; you might break it!" cried the witch. "Goodness is one of the most precious things in the world, and witches can hardly ever get hold of any. Give it to me!"

"Give it to *you!*" said Hop, "I should just think *not!* What would *you* do with a bottle of goodness I'd like to know!"

"I could make a wonderful spell!" said the witch. "Oh, give it to me, I beg of you!"

"We can't get into Fairyland if we give you our goodness," answered Hop; "so we're going to keep it."

"Then I shall keep the Princess!" shouted the witch in a temper.

The brownies looked at each other in despair. How *could* they give up their precious bottles when they had gone through such crowds of adventures to get them?

But they couldn't, COULDN'T let the darling brave little Princess be taken off by old Witch Green-eyes again. So with a sigh they knew they would have to give up their bottles of goodness.

"Very well, Witch Green-eyes," said Hop, in a sad little voice. "You shall have our three bottles if you will promise to let Peronel go free, and if you will promise, too, not to take us three brownies back with you."

The witch looked greedily at the three brightly coloured bottles.

"Give them to me!" she begged, stretching out her hand. "Peronel shall go free, and so shall you, too."

"Let us see the Princess safely into Fairyland first," said Hop. "And if you try to play us a trick, and snatch us all away and our bottles too, we will smash them so that they will be no use to you!"

"Yes, we *will*!" said Skip and Jump, thinking Hop was very clever and very brave.

"Let her go into the gates of Fairyland then," said the witch, "and give me the bottles afterwards!"

So Peronel ran quickly round the walls till she came to where the big gates of Fairyland stood tightly closed.

The brownies and the witch watched her beat at them with her little fists, and saw them open. There was a sound like a glad, astonished cry, and then the gates closed.

"They're shut again!" said Hop sadly.

"Quite shut," said Skip.

"Now give me the bottles," said the witch greedily.

They gave her their precious bottles, and

watched her whilst she ran chuckling to the magic carpet.

Then, whoo-oo-oo-oo! The carpet rose quickly into the air, and soon the witch had become nothing but a tiny bird-like speck in the sky.

The three brownies looked at each other.

"Our precious, precious bottles!" said Hop.

"We can't go back to Brownie Town!" said Skip in a choking voice.

"Still, we got Peronel back all right," said Jump, looking in all his pockets for a handkerchief.

Then a croak reminded them that their good friend the Dragon-bird was still near them.

They ran up to him and praised him and thanked him.

"I'm tired," he said, "so tired. Let's all cuddle up here and go to sleep. Then in the morning we will think of our future plans, for I shall never leave you now."

So the three forlorn little brownies cuddled together into the Dragon-bird, and soon fell fast asleep.

THEIR VERY LAST ADVENTURE OF ALL

THE sun went down, and still the brownies slept. Night came on, and still they lay sleeping. They were so tired out with excitement that they didn't even wake when the morning sun shone straight on to their faces.

But they *did* wake when they heard an excited little voice shouting into their ears, and felt someone tugging and pulling at their shoulders.

"Wake up, oh wake up! Oh, please, *do* wake up!" called a voice.

The brownies sat up with a jerk and looked at their awakener.

It was the Princess Peronel!

"Buttons and buttercups!" said Hop in the deepest astonishment. "What are *you* doing here?"

Peronel was dancing and skipping about in great excitement.

"Oh, I've told everyone all about you and your adventures!" she cried, "and the King and Queen are *so* glad to have me back. And I've told them how you found your goodness, and how you gave it up to old Witch Green-eyes to save me. And

I've told them I love you, and want you to come back to Fairyland, so's I can play with you sometimes. And they think you're brave and good, and WHAT DO YOU THINK?"

"What?" asked the brownies, who had been listening in amazement.

"There's a royal carriage coming to fetch you back to Brownie Town!" cried Peronel, hopping round with excitement. "It's coming in about two minutes, and I wanted to ride in it with you, so I've come out to tell you about it. I guessed you'd be here till the morning!"

"Good gracious!" said Hop, jumping up and trying to make his clothes look as if they hadn't been slept in. "But Peronel—how lovely of you to arrange it all!"

"I'm going to rescue *you* now, you see, to pay you back for you rescuing *me!*" laughed Peronel. "And the old Dragon-bird's coming too, of course. I told everyone how brave he was."

Well, there was such excitement among the five of them that they really didn't know what to do with themselves. They pulled their tunics straight, smoothed their hair, and brushed the dust from each other, a score of times, whilst the Dragon-bird preened every feather most proudly.

"There's the royal carriage!" shouted Hop

178

suddenly. Sure enough, there it was, coming out from the gates of Fairyland. Eight white horses drew it, and very grand and sparkling it looked. It drew up when the Princess stopped it.

In she got, and in got the three brownies. The Dragon-bird walked proudly along behind.

Then off set the royal carriage once more. It turned in through the gates of Fairyland, and the three brownies were so glad to be back again, that the tears ran down their faces in big trickles. The Princess was kept quite busy drying their eyes for them.

The carriage drove through Elfland, where hundreds of elves were waiting to cheer the carriage as it passed. Then it went through Cuckoo Wood, where scores and scores of woodland folk cheered them and ran after the carriage throwing roses and honeysuckle flowers.

Hop, Skip, and Jump were so happy that they really didn't know what to do.

"Fancy being back again!" said Hop.

"*Fancy* being back again!" echoed Skip.

"But just fancy it!" cried Jump in delight.

The Princess laughed. "It's just as nice for me as for you!" she said. "I was dreadfully homesick too!"

At last they reached Brownie Town. Hop,

Skip, and Jump knew every brownie who came running after the carriage, and called to their friends in joy.

"There's Gobo, dear old Gobo!" cried Hop.

"And Pinkie!" cried Skip.

"And Pippet, and Gruffles, and Hoppety!" cried Jump.

The Dragon-bird was very happy too. He walked solemnly along behind the carriage, and everyone stared at him in wonder, for they had never seen anything like him in Fairyland before.

"Here's the Palace!" said Peronel, as the royal carriage turned into the gates. It went up the long twisting drive, and at last stopped at the great shining doors of the Palace.

And on the steps to welcome the three brownies were their Majesties, the King and Queen.

"Welcome!" they cried. "Welcome to the brave little brownies, who rescued our daughter, and gave up their hard-won bottles of goodness for her safety. All your mischievous past is forgiven, for we know now that you are worthy of being brought back to Brownie Town! Welcome, too, to the brave Dragon-bird!"

"Hip-hip-hurrah!" shouted everyone.

"Don't let us have any more speeches," begged

Peronel. "Let's get to the feast. I'm sure the brownies are hungry!"

The brownies were really much too excited to feel hungry, but they were always ready for a feast.

And it *was* a feast. There were twenty different puddings, twelve different jellies, sixteen different blancmanges, and fifty different sorts of cake!

There was only one guest there who tried everything—and that was the Dragon-bird, who had really a most enormous appetite.

After the feast, the King ordered three cheers

for Hop, Skip, and Jump, and one big cheer for the Dragon-bird. Then he took a little key off his watch-chain and gave it to Hop.

"Here is the key of Crab-apple Cottage," he said kindly. "I expect you would like to go and get things straight there, wouldn't you?"

So off the brownies went to their dear little cottage, and except for dust, it was all just exactly as they had left it.

"Isn't it *lovely* to be home?" cried Hop, sitting on all the chairs one after another.

"*Isn't* it lovely to be home?" cried Skip, lying on all the beds in turn.

"Isn't it perfectly, absolutely lovely to be HOME?" cried Jump, winding up all the clocks joyfully.

"We'll never be bad again!" said Hop, solemnly.

"*Never*," said Skip.

"Never, never, *never*," said Jump.

So they settled down in their cottage again, and dusted and scrubbed, and made it as spick and span as could be. Everybody brought them flowers, and they put them in jugs and bowls, and made Crab-apple Cottage look sweeter than it had ever done before.

And once again the three brownies were happy —especially on Saturday afternoons, for then they always went to the Palace to play with the little Princess.

As for the Dragon-bird, he was much too fond of them all to go away. So they built him a nice big cage, and kept him for a pet. Every Saturday he takes them for a fine long fly in the air.

So if you happen to see a big, peculiar-looking bird flying quickly overhead one day, don't be alarmed. It will only be the Dragon-bird, taking his four passengers for their Saturday afternoon ride.

THE END

GOOD-BYE!

AND now the three brownies are happy once more,
  And the Princess is smiling and gay;
She often comes knocking at their cottage door
(Usually just about quarter-past four),
  And asks them to come out and play.

But first they have tea, and they eat jammy bread,
  While they talk just as fast as they can
Of the Vanishing Door and the Hob-Goblin Red,
Of the Very Wise Man with his very big head,
  And, of course, of the old Saucepan Man.

And Hop laughs to think of the worm they once
      met
  Who was in such a terrible hurry;
And Skip says he really will *never* forget
The time when the Green Railway Train was upset
  And put everyone in a flurry!

So they chatter and laugh while they finish their
    tea,
  Then they think they will go out to play;
And off they all clatter, as merry can be,
To take the old Dragon-bird out for a spree
  Away in the air, hip hurray!

They have a fine time in the sunny blue sky,
  And then come to earth with a bump.
And after that Peronel calls out "Good-bye!
Good-bye, dear old Dragon-bird; thanks for the
    fly,
  And good-bye to you, Hop, Skip and Jump!"

Also by Enid Blyton

A BOOK OF FAIRIES

"Welcome to Fairyland!"

Fairyland is full of magic and enchantment, and the lucky children in these stories have the most thrilling and surprising adventures with fairies, pixies, elves, brownies – and even witches and giants!

While Polly is swept off to the Land of Tiddly-winks by a magic kite, David pays a visit to Floppety Castle with Tom the Piper's son; meanwhile, Pat rescues Joan from the Land of Great Stupids, and Jack outwits a wicked spirit!

Enid Blyton

AMELIA JANE AGAIN!

"Amelia Jane, stop!" shouted all the toys in a rage. "Stop!"

Amelia Jane is a very bad doll. She's always making trouble for the other toys in the nursery. She catches them in a butterfly net, she hides their shoes down a mouse-hole, and she pelts them with snowballs. Sometimes the toys play tricks on Amelia Jane too, and then she promises to be good – but it's not long before she's naughty again!

Amelia Jane gets up to more mischief in

Naughty Amelia Jane!
Amelia Jane Gets Into Trouble!
Amelia Jane is Naughty Again!

Enid Blyton

MR MEDDLE'S MISCHIEF

"You're a tiresome, meddlesome creature, Mister Meddle!"

Mr Meddle is a very silly pixie. He's always getting in a muddle. He washes his hair with sherbet and cleans his teeth with glue; he feeds cake mixture to the pigs and worms to the budgies; he meddles with a conjuror's magic and drives an engine into the river. He just can't keep out of trouble!

You can have more fun with Mr Meddle in *Mr Meddle's Muddles*.

Enid Blyton

THE ADVENTURES OF THE WISHING-CHAIR

"Oh, Peter, to think we've got a magic chair – a wishing-chair!"

Mollie and Peter have a big secret; in their playroom is a magic Wishing-Chair which can grow wings and take them on flying adventures. They rescue Chinky the pixie from a giant's castle, visit Disappearing Island, and go to a party at Magician Greatheart's castle.

There's more Wishing-Chair magic in *The Wishing-Chair Again*.

Enid Blyton

THE WISHING-CHAIR AGAIN

"Fly home, chair, fly home!" commanded Peter.

Mollie and Peter and their pixie friend, Chinky, have great adventures flying off in the magic Wishing-Chair. They meet magicians, witches, goblins and enchanters; they visit the Land of Spells and the Island of Surprises; they rescue a naughty brownie from Mister Grim's school for Bad Brownies, and the poor Wishing-Chair has its wings cut off by the Slipperies!

You can have more fun with the Wishing-Chair in *The Adventures of the Wishing-Chair*.

A Selected List of Fiction from Mammoth

While every effort is made to keep prices low, it is sometimes necessary to increase prices at short notice. Mammoth Books reserves the right to show new retail prices on covers which may differ from those previously advertised in the text or elsewhere.

The prices shown below were correct at the time of going to press.

☐	416 13972 8	**Why the Whales Came**	Michael Morpurgo	£2.50
☐	7497 0034 3	**My Friend Walter**	Michael Morpurgo	£2.50
☐	7497 0035 1	**The Animals of Farthing Wood**	Colin Dann	£2.99
☐	7497 0136 6	**I Am David**	Anne Holm	£2.50
☐	7497 0139 0	**Snow Spider**	Jenny Nimmo	£2.50
☐	7497 0140 4	**Emlyn's Moon**	Jenny Nimmo	£2.25
☐	7497 0344 X	**The Haunting**	Margaret Mahy	£2.25
☐	416 96850 3	**Catalogue of the Universe**	Margaret Mahy	£1.95
☐	7497 0051 3	**My Friend Flicka**	Mary O'Hara	£2.99
☐	7497 0079 3	**Thunderhead**	Mary O'Hara	£2.99
☐	7497 0219 2	**Green Grass of Wyoming**	Mary O'Hara	£2.99
☐	416 13722 9	**Rival Games**	Michael Hardcastle	£1.99
☐	416 13212 X	**Mascot**	Michael Hardcastle	£1.99
☐	7497 0126 9	**Half a Team**	Michael Hardcastle	£1.99
☐	416 08812 0	**The Whipping Boy**	Sid Fleischman	£1.99
☐	7497 0033 5	**The Lives of Christopher Chant**	Diana Wynne-Jones	£2.50
☐	7497 0164 1	**A Visit to Folly Castle**	Nina Beachcroft	£2.25

All these books are available at your bookshop or newsagent, or can be ordered direct from the publisher. Just tick the titles you want and fill in the form below.

Mandarin Paperbacks, Cash Sales Department, PO Box 11, Falmouth, Cornwall TR10 9EN.

Please send cheque or postal order, no currency, for purchase price quoted and allow the following for postage and packing:

UK   80p for the first book, 20p for each additional book ordered to a maximum charge of £2.00.

BFPO   80p for the first book, 20p for each additional book.

Overseas   £1.50 for the first book, £1.00 for the second and 30p for each additional book
including Eire   thereafter.

NAME (Block letters) ....

ADDRESS ....

....

....